MOUTHPIECE

SELECTED FICTION WORKS BY L. RON HUBBARD

FANTASY

The Case of the Friendly Corpse

Death's Deputy

Fear

The Ghoul

The Indigestible Triton

Slaves of Sleep & The Masters of Sleep

Typewriter in the Sky

The Ultimate Adventure

SCIENCE FICTION

Battlefield Earth

The Conquest of Space

The End Is Not Yet

Final Blackout

The Kilkenny Cats

The Kingslayer

The Mission Earth Dekalogy*

Ole Doc Methuselah

To the Stars

ADVENTURE

The Hell Job series

WESTERN

Buckskin Brigades

Empty Saddles

Guns of Mark Jardine

Hot Lead Payoff

A full list of L. Ron Hubbard's novellas and short stories is provided at the back.

*Dekalogy—a group of ten volumes

L. RON HUBBARD

MOUTHPIECE

Published by
Galaxy Press, LLC
7051 Hollywood Boulevard, Suite 200
Hollywood, CA 90028

Printed in the United States of America.

ISBN-10 1-59212-356-2
ISBN-13 978-1-59212-356-8

Library of Congress Control Number: 2007903529

CONTENTS

FOREWORD

STORIES FROM PULP FICTION'S GOLDEN AGE

AND it *was* a golden age.

The 1930s and 1940s were a vibrant, seminal time for a gigantic audience of eager readers, probably the largest per capita audience of readers in American history. The magazine racks were chock-full of publications with ragged trims, garish cover art, cheap brown pulp paper, low cover prices—and the most excitement you could hold in your hands.

"Pulp" magazines, named for their rough-cut, pulpwood paper, were a vehicle for more amazing tales than Scheherazade could have told in a million and one nights. Set apart from higher-class "slick" magazines, printed on fancy glossy paper with quality artwork and superior production values, the pulps were for the "rest of us," adventure story after adventure story for people who liked to *read.* Pulp fiction authors were no-holds-barred entertainers—real storytellers. They were more interested in a thrilling plot twist, a horrific villain or a white-knuckle adventure than they were in lavish prose or convoluted metaphors.

The sheer volume of tales released during this wondrous golden age remains unmatched in any other period of literary history—hundreds of thousands of published stories in over nine hundred different magazines. Some titles lasted only an issue or two; many magazines succumbed to paper shortages during World War II, while others endured for decades yet. Pulp fiction remains as a treasure trove of stories you can read, stories you can love, stories you can remember. The stories were driven by plot and character, with grand heroes, terrible villains, beautiful damsels (often in distress), diabolical plots, amazing places, breathless romances. The readers wanted to be taken beyond the mundane, to live adventures far removed from their ordinary lives—and the pulps rarely failed to deliver.

In that regard, pulp fiction stands in the tradition of all memorable literature. For as history has shown, good stories are much more than fancy prose. William Shakespeare, Charles Dickens, Jules Verne, Alexandre Dumas—many of the greatest literary figures wrote their fiction for the readers, not simply literary colleagues and academic admirers. And writers for pulp magazines were no exception. These publications reached an audience that dwarfed the circulations of today's short story magazines. Issues of the pulps were scooped up and read by over thirty million avid readers each month.

Because pulp fiction writers were often paid no more than a cent a word, they had to become prolific or starve. They also had to write aggressively. As Richard Kyle, publisher and editor of *Argosy,* the first and most long-lived of the pulps, so pointedly explained: "The pulp magazine writers, the best of them, worked for markets that did not write for critics or attempt to satisfy timid advertisers. Not having to answer to anyone other than their readers, they wrote about human beings on the edges of the unknown, in those new lands the future would explore. They wrote for what we would become, not for what we had already been."

Some of the more lasting names that graced the pulps include H. P. Lovecraft, Edgar Rice Burroughs, Robert E. Howard, Max Brand, Louis L'Amour, Elmore Leonard, Dashiell Hammett, Raymond Chandler, Erle Stanley Gardner, John D. MacDonald, Ray Bradbury, Isaac Asimov, Robert Heinlein—and, of course, L. Ron Hubbard.

In a word, he was among the most prolific and popular writers of the era. He was also the most enduring—hence this series—and certainly among the most legendary. It all began only months after he first tried his hand at fiction, with L. Ron Hubbard tales appearing in *Thrilling Adventures, Argosy, Five-Novels Monthly, Detective Fiction Weekly, Top-Notch, Texas Ranger, War Birds, Western Stories,* even *Romantic Range.* He could write on any subject, in any genre, from jungle explorers to deep-sea divers, from G-men and gangsters, cowboys and flying aces to mountain climbers, hard-boiled detectives and spies. But he really began to shine when he turned his talent to science fiction and fantasy of which he authored nearly fifty novels or novelettes to forever change the shape of those genres.

Following in the tradition of such famed authors as Herman Melville, Mark Twain, Jack London and Ernest Hemingway, Ron Hubbard actually lived adventures that his own characters would have admired—as an ethnologist among primitive tribes, as prospector and engineer in hostile climes, as a captain of vessels on four oceans. He even wrote a series of articles for *Argosy,* called "Hell Job," in which he lived and told of the most dangerous professions a man could put his hand to.

Finally, and just for good measure, he was also an accomplished photographer, artist, filmmaker, musician and educator. But he was first and foremost a *writer,* and that's the L. Ron Hubbard we come to know through the pages of this volume.

This library of Stories from the Golden Age presents the best of L. Ron Hubbard's fiction from the heyday of storytelling, the Golden Age of the pulp magazines. In these eighty volumes, readers are treated to a full banquet of 153 stories, a kaleidoscope of tales representing every imaginable genre: science fiction, fantasy, western, mystery, thriller, horror, even romance—action of all kinds and in all places.

Because the pulps themselves were printed on such inexpensive paper with high acid content, issues were not meant to endure. As the years go by, the original issues of every pulp from *Argosy* through *Zeppelin Stories* continue crumbling into brittle, brown dust. This library preserves the L. Ron Hubbard tales from that era, presented with a distinctive look that brings back the nostalgic flavor of those times.

L. Ron Hubbard's Stories from the Golden Age has something for every taste, every reader. These tales will return you to a time when fiction was good clean entertainment and the most fun a kid could have on a rainy afternoon or the best thing an adult could enjoy after a long day at work.

Pick up a volume, and remember what reading is supposed to be all about. Remember curling up with a *great story.*

—Kevin J. Anderson

KEVIN J. ANDERSON *is the author of more than ninety critically acclaimed works of speculative fiction, including The Saga of Seven Suns, the continuation of the Dune Chronicles with Brian Herbert, and his* New York Times *bestselling novelization of L. Ron Hubbard's* Ai! Pedrito!

MOUTHPIECE

MOUTHPIECE

IT had been a long time since Mat Lawrence had stood upon the corner of a city street; and he found that the sound of traffic—that nerve-tearing clamor of bells, horns, motors and flat-wheeled streetcars—was a foreign and intolerable thing. For three years he had worked in a silent desert, building a mammoth power dam. The loudest noise had been a coyote's howl at midnight and the swiftest movement that of a buzzard a mile in the air.

With his usual self-sufficiency he did not know that his dusty boots and battered Stetson made him conspicuous; he only remarked to himself that it was strange how pale the people of his former city had become—for Mat and his engineers had been turned walnut brown by the blazing desert sun.

New buildings, odd cars, new parks—he caught himself wondering if he—the son of Lawrence, the gangster—had ever belonged to this world of sound and steel. Then he caught the name of a building across the street and he reverted to his mission.

In direct contradiction to his tremendous height and bulk, he slid swiftly and easily through the ranks of speeding cars.

He arrived at the building's entrance to soar upwards to the eleventh floor. His leather heels clanged in the marble corridor and he swung back the door marked: "C. G. Swartz, Attorney at Law."

With his eyes fixed on a man who sat indolently at an ornate desk in the second room, he failed to notice that a protesting office boy was attempting to hold the gate. Lawrence walked on through, to come to a deliberate stop beside the desk.

Behind a scattered array of papers which lapped over the edges of an old-fashioned sand blotting box, Swartz looked up. A startled expression attempted to hide in his dark eyes; his round, hairless head gleamed as shiny as though newly polished.

"Harumph!" coughed Swartz. "I didn't expect—"

"No!" drawled Mat. "You probably didn't. Why in hell didn't you wire me that Dad was dead?"

His poise regained, Swartz pulled his beefy length out of the swivel chair and offered a hand which Mat shook dubiously.

"I didn't think it was necessary, Mr. Lawrence. And besides, telegrams cost money."

"Sure they cost money. Why so careful about Dad's finances all of a sudden? You didn't use to worry about it! I remember one case where—"

"Now, now, now!" cut in Swartz. "You don't fully understand. Didn't you read the letter I sent you?"

"Why, I guess I did. What's that got to do with it?"

Seated and securely entrenched behind his fancy desk, Swartz assumed a consoling air. "My boy, your father died penniless. There was neither will nor estate."

"What?" demanded Mat. "At last report, Swartz, he had a cool million sacked away. That's a hell of a wad to fade!"

He slapped the Stetson on the desk, where it eddied dust. "If Dad died broke, he died broke. I'd like to know why; but what I really want to know is every detail of his dying. I don't want news talk, I want facts. You've got them. You've always got them. Dad paid you out dough in six figures many a time, and I guess it still ought to buy the dope."

"As for your father's fortune," murmured Swartz, "I only know that he invested heavily in worthless securities. He was an impulsive man, and though I often attempted to advise him, he would never listen to me."

Mat snorted. "Probably not, and I don't blame him. Now, I want to know what happened."

"You can never quite tell in this game, Mr. Lawrence. You know that."

"Come on, Swartz, quit stalling."

Swartz made a tent out of his fat fingers and then moved them up to tug at his lower lip, his eyes warily regarding Mat. "All right, I'll tell you. Rat-Face O'Connell was on his trail. Your father had the dyeing and cleaning protection racket of this town and Rat-Face and his boys didn't like it. So, one night they went up to your father's apartment, shot down the guards and took Lawrence for a ride. That's the story."

Mat probed into the man's face as though searching for flaws. "Rat-Face O'Connell, eh?" He looked musingly into the palm of his hand as if it were a textbook. "Rat-Face O'Connell. All right, where does he hang around?"

"Oh no, no!" cried Swartz.

"Oh yes, yes!" disputed Mat. "Where can I find him, now—tonight?"

"But . . . but," blubbered Swartz. "It's . . . it's suicide, Mr. Lawrence. I can't let you do it." He whipped out a polka-dot handkerchief and mopped at his brow as though the idea had turned the room into a furnace. "You'd better get out and leave this thing alone!"

"I suppose I'm a yellowbelly. Like the rest of you guys, eh?" Mat threw a twisted smile at Swartz. "Well, you're wrong. If you think anybody can bump my dad and then get off scot-free, you're cockeyed as hell."

His square jaw jutted out and his eyes were the size of match heads. "I'm looking to get Mr. Rat-Face and make him talk. Talk, get me? He'll burn for that night's work, or by God, I'll take him to hell with me."

"Wheeoo!" breathed Swartz, mopping ever harder. He fanned himself with the silk, leaning back in the chair. It was as though he had cooled his legal brain, for he suddenly crouched forward, confidential and wise. "How much money have you got, Mr. Lawrence?"

"Oh, I see!" snapped Mat. "I've got to pay for the dope."

"No," purred Swartz, "you haven't. I'm going to give you the address. The dough is for a couple of your father's gorillas to go with you. You remember them. Petey and Blake."

Mat sought for the answer in his palm and after several moments of concentrated searching, looked up. "All right. I've got five hundred bucks. That will cover Petey, Blake and a car. You're going to lend me a gat."

"Fine." Swartz leaned back again. "I'll send them around at seven to your hotel. Where are you stopping?"

"Oh, I guess the Savoy is as good as any. Now," he got up

to leave, "where are my dad's papers? I want to read them over and find out what the score was."

Swartz gave Mat a sad stare. "The papers were all taken by O'Connell and his boys. He didn't leave anything with me, ever."

Mat frowned and then walked to the door, placing his huge hand on the knob. "I'll be back and see you tomorrow, Swartz, if I live to tell the yarn."

Sharply at seven a black sedan stood courteously at the entrance of the Savoy Hotel, two men in the front seat. Mat Lawrence loomed out of the lighted doorway, towering over the gilt-frogged doorman, and looked into the car. He saw Petey first. "Hello, Petey. Hello, Blake."

Petey was mostly chest and his head resembled nothing so much as a shoe box sunk into his torso—green buttons for eyes and a ragged knife gash for a mouth. Blake was oily and sleek, his hair glistening more than his patent leather shoes, and his black eyes shinier than either. They gave Mat a heartless "Hello" and glanced at each other.

"Get in back, mugs," commanded Mat. "I'm driving."

Grudgingly, shying away from the bright lights of the entrance as though they stung, Petey and Blake squirmed out and slunk into the back seat.

Three sizes too big for the seat, Mat crumped the gears and stabbed the headlights out into the blur of traffic. "Where do we go?"

Petey leaned forward, his voice rasping like a saw in mahogany. "Head straight out this street, bo. I'll put ya wise to the turns." He glanced at Blake before he sat back and Blake nodded, his lips sliding into a knowing smile as though well oiled.

With a turn here and a curve there, the sedan went on through the glaring city until the house windows were more dimly lighted and the houses themselves seemed to exude darkness. Mat found it hard to distinguish streets from alleys.

"Hey, Petey," he called over his shoulder. "Where's the gun Swartz sent?"

Petey slid an automatic pistol across the rear seat. Mat looked at the blue glint and then shoved the weapon into his coat, to slip out the clip and find that it was fully loaded.

"Thanks, Petey." He glanced up into the rearview mirror. "Say, what the hell are you smiling about?"

"Oh, things," rasped Petey. "You turn down this next one."

Suddenly uncomfortable as if he were hearing fingernails scraping over a blackboard, Mat turned the designated corner and found that he was leaving the last of the houses behind him.

He humped over the wheel, speeding up.

"Say, Petey," he hurled over his shoulder. "Were you in at Dad's finish?"

Leaning forward, Petey obliged. "Nope, I arrived about ten minutes afterwards. This Rat-Face O'Connell had cleared out with most of the papers and all the loose jack. I been itchin' ta get my mitts on him ever since."

He pointed with a dirty finger. "Ya turn down that next road there. The little one."

"Okay." Mat did as he was directed. "This bird sure lives a

helluva ways out, doesn't he? Listen, I'm going to drive right up in front of the house. You two birds circle around back and try to get in that way. After that we'll see what we'll see. Get me?"

"Sure," said Petey.

"If I'm right, this Rat-Face is a rotten shot. And I want him alive, get that? Alive! He's going to burn, see?"

"Sure," said Petey.

"Say!" Mat sat up suddenly and slowed down. "This is the city dump!"

"Sure!" said Petey. "Slow down and stop." He pressed a gat into Mat's ear where it bored viciously. "You didn't know it, bo, but you was takin' yerself fer a ride!"

Mat stiffened, involuntarily reaching for the foot brake. The gun in his ear was a round, hard snarl. Then, still moving at thirty miles an hour, he stamped down on the gas. "Yeah? Well, Petey, if you blow me to hell now, you'll go along too!"

"Slow down!" screamed Blake. "You'll kill all of us!"

Petey drew the pistol away from Mat's head, staring beadily at the treacherous, curving road over which they were hurtling. "Jeeze! Quit, fer God's sakes!"

Mat's square face was savage. He jerked the car around the twisting turns as though he could have picked it out of the road by the steering wheel and whirled it around his head. The headlights clashed on cans and broken glass, throwing themselves over the edge of a twenty-foot drop to the right of the car.

Petey was frozen with terror as he watched that bank full of darkness. He knew that if he shot Mat then and there, he could never snatch the wheel in time to save the car and his own hide.

Watching the cans and glass ahead of them, Mat's eyes were the shade, temperature and density of ice. His left hand sneaked away from the wheel and his fingers closed over the door catch. Holding his breath he saw a left turn dart around ahead. With a lunge he twisted the car wheel to the right and sprang out and away, to light doubled up and rolling on the sharp, scorching earth.

The sedan careened, flopped over to the right. Its headlights whacked up and then gracefully swept down into emptiness. A brittle crunch was followed by splintering glass and a scream.

Mat had stopped rolling. Before the crash had ceased to echo, he was on his feet, lunging toward the embankment after the car, his automatic almost engulfed in his huge hand. Cans crunched under his boots and cinders scattered away when he came to a halt above the sedan.

One headlight, still burning, pointed up at him, though the car was on its tattered back, its engine coughing gradually into silence. Mat's jaw was thrust out and a smile pulled up one corner of his mouth. Unthinkingly, he stood directly in the beam from the headlight.

Flame spurted from one side of the car and lead whispered past Mat's hand. A second flash came from the right; but the target had dived down and now lay at full length on the piles of ashes.

Coolly, Mat brought up the pistol and sighted on a saffron ribbon below. He squeezed the trigger with marksmanlike perfection, but the hammer clicked emptily.

"What the hell?" bellowed Mat, pulling back the slide for a second try. The same result snicked in his ears. He started to throw the gun to one side and then changed his mind, placing it carefully in his torn pocket.

Inching along the dark rim, he crawled out of range of the lights and then slipped over the embankment to slide silently down to the car's level. Now, in back of it, he could see a silhouette in the headlight's glare and recognized Petey, tensed on one elbow, his gun trained on the bank above.

Patiently, as though he had nothing if not time, Mat crawled quietly along until he could almost touch the shattered back of the inverted sedan. The smell of leaking gas was in his dilated nostrils and Petey's silhouette, even down to the poised gun, fully occupied his calm eyes. For a full minute Mat lay still, looking at Petey, debating whether or not to use his gun butt for a sap. But the thought was somehow jangling.

Creeping forward he came up beside Petey, almost level with his shoulder.

Petey heard the rustling sound of cloth against cinders and whispered out of the corner of his mouth, "Did we hit him, Blake?"

"No," whispered Mat. He grabbed Petey by the scruff of the neck and jerked him upright, bringing a sledgehammer fist viciously into the shoe-box face. "No," repeated Mat, dropping the limp figure, "you didn't."

"What's that?" called Blake from the other side of the car. "What'd you say?"

Mat fumbled around until he found Petey's automatic. He grasped it tightly before standing up. "You," he bellowed, "had better toss away that toy you're holding and holler uncle!"

Lead smashed through the car from the other side, whining away across the city dump. And lead went back through, three times, to stop abruptly, eliciting a shrill scream.

Mat carefully snapped on the pistol's safety catch and then walked over to the embankment. By the car's light, he found a piece of rusty iron wire looped out of the ashes. He pulled it to him amid a clatter and crunch of rusty tin cans and then strode back to the car.

Petey received the first treatment, and soon he was wired tightly, propped against the front bumper of the sedan, his head wearily dropped on his chest.

As Blake was secured he moaned aloud.

"Shut up," ordered Mat. "You aren't hurt. Those two punctures won't do any more than let some of the grease out of you." He gave the wire a final twist and then stood back to appreciate his handiwork.

Petey came to with a yell and a squirm which subsided instantly as he saw the bulk of Mat squatting on his heels before them.

"Now that the congregation is assembled, boys," purred Mat, "we might as well hold a confession. They tell me it's good for the soul, though that probably lets you two out. I want the lowdown on the higher-ups."

Green eyes and black eyes stubbornly glared at him. Two sets of twitching lips tried to be firm and unrelenting.

"So," remarked Mat, "you won't talk. Well, there's plenty of time." He took the automatic which Petey had given him earlier in the evening and extracted a cartridge from it.

Listening intently, he shook the shell close to his ear and then grunted. With a penknife and a hard cinder he carefully extracted the steel-jacketed lead and poured the contents of the shell into his hand.

"Sand!" Mat jiggled his hand, looking at the white particles. "Now, I wonder what bright boy thought that up."

He found Blake's pistol by the car and with this in his right hand and Petey's in his left, he backed away in the headlight's glare, hefting the two weapons suggestively. "You're sure you don't want to talk?"

Silence came from the bumper in spite of uneasy squirming.

"Well, I haven't had any target practice for some time." Mat backed away until he was well up on the embankment.

Carefully sighting on the first number of the license plate between the two gunmen, Mat squeezed the trigger, expertly puncturing the numeral.

"Now," he purred, "we'll skip a number, and then another, and then the next one catches Petey between the eyes. That leaves Blake to talk. If he doesn't want to, I go back the way I came and take off each of Blake's ears." He raised his left hand and ventilated the designated numeral.

Just as he was bringing down his right gun, Petey wailed, "I'll talk! I'll squeal! Honest-to-God, I'll talk! Don't shoot!"

Carefully sighting on the first number of the license plate between the two gunmen, Mat squeezed the trigger, expertly puncturing the numeral.

Mat sat down in front of him, bending an attentive ear to Petey's babble.

"Rat-Face found out about it!" Petey moaned. "He's got plenty on me and he said if I didn't, he'd squawk to the bulls. I didn't wanna drill ya! Honest, I didn't! But he made me. He told me to give you that phony gun in case you got suspicious." Petey rambled on with details.

Mat got to his feet and bound up the two bullet holes in Blake's arm and side. He fixed the wire so that it held the two gunmen together and left long, trailing ends. Taking the two wires in his left hand, and a gun in his right, Mat said, "Giddap!"

Although it was a long walk back to the edge of town, Mat's stride was as strong as ever when the first lamppost was reached.

But Petey and Blake dragged woeful heels, as though every step was the last.

A taxi came to their rescue and whirred through town toward a residential section. Stately lawns sloped primly back toward overbearing mansions, and huge cars were parked at the curb. When their taxi braked before an especially imposing home, Mat herded his two wards to the sidewalk where they drooped, paid the driver and marched down a perfectly landscaped expanse, coming to a halt before the castle-like door.

Listening to the sound of an orchestra inside, Mat read "C. G. Swartz" on the doorplate and then rang the bell.

The butler who answered was politely amazed at the spectacle on the veranda. "I'm sorry, gentlemen, but Mr.

Swartz is giving a party and no visitors are to be admitted." He bowed slightly from the hips.

"Tough," remarked Mat, and the butler found himself sprawled on the floor, the lights spinning above him.

Swartz's party was the height of elegance. Men who were unmistakably judges and politicians, and women who were undoubtedly snobbish, swirled about to the tune of a twelve-piece orchestra. Mat lifted one eyebrow at the colorful sight and then looked about him.

A secure coat-hook caught and held his attention. He twisted his two wires together in a loop, to hoist his prisoners off the floor and leave them obscenely dangling in midair.

Nonchalantly oblivious of his laced boots and generally secondhand condition, Mat stepped into the ballroom. Grimly he looked about, attempting to single out Swartz.

A sudden motion caught Mat's attention and he saw Swartz, tipping forward as though he was about to fall.

The hairless head was quivering with surprise, and the black eyes were two beads of terror.

Mat looked across the room at Swartz, his square face sliding into a cold smile. "Good evening, Mr. Swartz," he called.

And with long, effortless strides, his leather heels crashing through the stillness of the room, not minding the unanimity of eyes which were disdainfully upon him, Mat came close to Swartz. His eyes bored into the spherical blob of surprised flesh.

"Sorry to trouble you, Swartz," said Mat, "but I thought

you'd like to know that Petey squealed." His tone was impersonal, his eyes watchful.

The shiny face turned yellow, then dead white, and Swartz tottered back. His hand darted to his hip, and terror shone in his eyes—animal terror which gave no thought to anything but the impulse to kill.

Mat's hand shot out and caught the wrist, doubling the arm back with a savage jerk. Mat's voice crashed through the room like a cannon shot.

"You're clever, Mouthpiece. But not clever enough! When you shot Dad, you thought I'd clear out, didn't you? You didn't count on my coming back, did you?" He wrenched the arm again and beads of sweat darted out against the lawyer's gray forehead.

Men in evening clothes were pulling at Mat's arms, trying to pry him away from Swartz. Voices were blended in an excited, hysterical roar.

Mat whipped about, still holding to Swartz, brushing away the men as though they were made of paper.

"Get back! This is my party!" The sheer strength of his voice seemed physical and the crowd swept away, staring, once more silent.

Turning to Swartz, his eyes deadly, Mat snapped, "Talk, Mouthpiece. Go on and talk. You got plenty to tell and no doubt your friends will want to hear about it." With a slow smile he reached into his pocket and brought forth a folded sheaf of papers which he crackled in front of Swartz.

"See these? Well, they're signed confessions by your little

pals Petey and Blake. They squealed, see? Turned state's evidence. I got it here in black-and-white that it was your bullet which knocked off my dad!"

"It's a lie!" screamed Swartz, pitiful in his terror. "It's a lie. They did it for me! They did it and I can prove it! I had a party that night and anybody'll tell you I didn't do it! I didn't, hear me? I didn't."

The silence of the room deepened. Swartz stared wildly about, suddenly realizing what he had done. His knees crumpled under him and his head rolled forward, shining in the colored lights. But Mat grabbed the front of his coat and held him up, shaking him.

Mat's words whipped and lashed about Swartz. "You had me taken for a ride tonight. Gave me a dud gun and planted your gorillas on me. Sent me after a right guy! Now, what have you got to say?"

He shook the lawyer savagely, holding the dangling feet clear off the floor. "Where's the cash you stole off my dad?"

Swartz gurgled and looked up, beaten, whipped. "All right, Lawrence. All right." His voice was dead and his eyes were glued to the papers Mat still held before him. "I'll talk!"

He wailed suddenly. "I'll talk! But don't shake me! Set me down!"

"Talk!" snapped Mat.

"The key's in my pocket!" cried Swartz. "The key to the safe-deposit box at the First National! It's all there! Every penny of it's there!"

"You're witnesses," Mat said to the crowd, dropping Swartz to the yellow hardwood floor. He ransacked the pockets of the lawyer's dress suit and brought to light a ring of keys. "Which one?"

"That one," moaned Swartz, pointing.

As Mat extracted the designated key from the ring, a tall, dignified gentleman with white hair tapped him on the shoulder.

"I'm Judge Halloway," said the man. "I can act in an official capacity. You have reference to the Lawrence murder, is that right?"

"Yes," affirmed Mat, getting to his feet. "I got the goods on Swartz and those two lads outside. They tried to bump me tonight."

With a glance at the heap of broadcloth and palsied flesh which was Swartz, Halloway drew Mat to one side. "You'd better give me those confessions."

"What confessions?" Mat was puzzled for an instant and then grinned, looking down at the sheaf in his hand. "Oh! These aren't anything. They're just some estimates for mules to haul dirt, out at the power project."

"But," faltered Halloway, "how did you know that Swartz was guilty?"

Mat grinned and pulled out the automatic which Petey had given him. "Swartz gave me this through a gangster named Petey. He thought I'd try to pull some rough stuff and use it; and as long as I'd asked for it, he gave it to me."

He slipped a cartridge out of the clip and quickly bit the lead out of the brass shell with his teeth, to pour white sand in his palm. "He had to give me dud cartridges and he was afraid I'd investigate too soon.

"You see this white sand in my palm? Well, Petey claimed that another mobster bribed him to plant this gun on me and take me for a ride. But this white sand says differently. Have you ever noticed that old sand blotting box on Swartz's desk?"

"Yes," admitted Halloway.

"Well, this is the same kind of sand." Mat bounced it in his hand. "If my mineralogy doesn't tell me wrong, it's identical—and there's very little in this part of the world. Then, too, see that black grain there? That's ink."

"Then," concluded Halloway, "he replaced the powder in the cartridges with the sand from the box on his desk. Well, well, and well. But that evidence isn't necessary. I've enough on him to bring him to trial. I'd better take him into custody now. Drop around to the station tomorrow and we'll get everything straight."

Mat juggled the mound of sand in his palm and carefully pocketed the faked bullets for future evidence. He gave the room a brief sweep with smiling eyes and then slowly made his way out into the hall where Petey and Blake still dangled from the coat hooks. They hung there like abandoned marionettes from some wild apache puppet show, their faces set in an emotionless, fatalistic stare.

Grinning now, in appreciation of the joke, Mat stopped before them. He presented the little white mound in his palm, beside which he had placed the key to the safe-deposit box which held a fortune.

"You know," remarked Mat Lawrence, "it takes sand to get along in this world. But," he made the mound jump again, "your boss in there has just a little too much."

And Petey and Blake, with their hard, emotionless eyes, watched him saunter out through the ornate doorway—back to a world where buzzards flew and coyotes howled and wheels were waiting to be turned in the construction of a mammoth power dam.

FLAME CITY

CHAPTER ONE

SIFTING EVIDENCE

THE shrieks and moans of sirens greeted Tom Delaney as he swung into the corridor which led to his father's office. He paused for a moment to listen, feeling somewhat ill at ease and out of place.

To a detective-sergeant, fires were the business of another world. But his father, old Blaze Delaney, chief of the fire-eaters, had called him and Tom Delaney had responded, wondering just how a detective could hope to extricate a fireman from an intricate web of circumstances.

Before Detective-Sergeant Tom Delaney could knock, his father swooped out of his office, drawing on slicker and helmet as he ran. Blaze Delaney's fire-reddened face was set and hard and his smoke-stung eyes caught and held the image of his son.

"Another one!" he shouted, his mustache bristling. "Come on!"

The detective swung into line, hard put to keep up with the racing old man. When Blaze Delaney swung into the red car without pausing and sent it hurtling away from the curb, his son was forced to catch a precarious hold on the side, swinging from there into the seat.

"What's up?" asked Tom.

"What's up, be hanged!" bellowed Blaze Delaney. "There's

plenty up, and if you didn't keep your big ears so close to the woes of petty thieves you'd know that your old man was about to be thrown out."

Blaze Delaney thrown out? The detective blinked and tried to imagine such a circumstance. As long as he could remember, his father had been lord of the city's fires. His father was an immovable institution, a character of great repute.

Tom Delaney watched the old fire-eater's anger vent itself against the traffic. He always drove his own cars, did Blaze, for the good reason that he could drive faster than anyone on the department's rolls.

"I've noticed," began Tom, cautiously, "that we've been having more fires than usual, but—"

"More fires than usual! Humph! Young fellow, we've had two hundred and fifty percent more fires in the past two months than in any other corresponding period. If you don't know that, you don't even read the newspapers. Right now the Tyler Department Store is burning, and it's a concrete building that can't burn."

He went around a corner on something less than two wheels, missed a pair of streetcars and gave a taxi driver the scare of his life. The automatic siren was wailing, almost drowning conversation in the coupe.

"But," said the detective, "why should you be kicked out just because—"

"That's why I sent for you. You're supposed to be good at riddles."

"You mean you think it's arson on a big scale?"

Blaze Delaney grunted loudly. "I don't think it, I know it."

Tom's dark eyebrows went up and his shoulders moved in the slightest kind of a shrug.

"I thought you had a special department which investigated such things," he murmured.

"That's what you think."

"Well, I'm telling you this, Dad. I don't know anything about fires and what starts 'em. But if you're in trouble and you think I can be of help, here I am."

"Good," said the chief. "That's what I wanted you to say. If this thing doesn't stop, I'm out of a job and my reputation is wrecked. Well, there's the fire." Blaze Delaney rocketed up to the lines and jumped out.

"Confound that Number Three. I told 'em to wait for me before they—" And then a swelling wall of smoke swallowed both the chief and his words, and the detective-sergeant was left with his riddle.

Tyler's Department Store was a welter of shooting smoke and snapping flames. The entire first floor was filled with lightning-like tongues, against which the thin streams of water seemed fragile and aimless.

Tom Delaney sat still and watched the toiling firemen at their seemingly hopeless task. Dusk was falling and lending color to the blaze. The flames began to recede slowly and sullenly under the onslaught of water and chemicals.

The detective looked up to see a tall, incredibly thin man approaching the red coupe.

"Where's the old man?" asked the newcomer.

The detective shrugged. "In there eating smoke, like he always is."

"You're his son, that right? I'm Blackford, head of the Investigation Department."

Tom Delaney shook the limp hand with a feeling of distaste.

"Three girls must have sizzled," continued Blackford. "I can't account for them. Too bad."

"Looks like arson, doesn't it?" said the detective.

"Don't know. I never can tell until I get inside. There was a garage under the first floor and I think we'll find it started from oily waste. It usually does. Some mechanic gets careless with a cigarette butt and zowie, there you are."

"When do you investigate?" asked Tom.

"Soon as it cools down. That'll be in about another hour. Why, you figuring on sticking around?"

"Do you mind if I do?"

"No," said Blackford. "Glad to have you. Then you can okay my report." He started away into the crowd, his eyes whipping about as though still searching for the fire chief.

Almost an hour later, Blaze Delaney came back to his car. He was black with soot and smoke, and dripping from innumerable encounters with lashing streams of water. He had an odor about him like that of wet ashes.

"Hell," roared the old man. "There's another one across town. Residence."

Tom whistled. "I'll stay here and go over the ruins with Blackford."

"Know him? That's good. Fine fellow, Blackford; he'll show you the ropes if you want to learn. Go on, pile out. I'm in a hurry."

Tom Delaney piled out and stood on the soaked asphalt

watching the red coupe go screaming out of sight. Engines and hose carts were pulling out in its wake, carrying their cargoes of red-eyed, dripping men who swore wearily as they realized that the night's work promised no respite.

Blackford was standing just outside the gutted door of the department store, playing a flashlight over the black interior. He turned the beam on the detective.

"Hello! I was hoping you'd be along. It looks safe enough inside, but don't move anything. That second floor looks like it's sagging in spots."

Lazy spirals of steam were rising up from the ravaged counters to hang in the air like a choking poisonous gas. Goods were heaped in sullen, charred piles which dripped gray water. Two men in raincoats stood dismally beside the wall, looking at the chaos.

"Hello, Blackford," said one. "Hope you get this thing figured out in a hurry. There's a hundred thousand in goods insurance alone."

"Yeah," grunted the other. "You would be worried about your blamed insurance. What about my company, that's paying all this? If we find out it's arson, it's going to go hard with somebody. Look alive, Blackford." Slowly he trudged out of the shambles into the flickering glitter of the street lights.

"That first one was Tyler himself," said the investigator. "The other guy was Morley, of Graysons' Insurance Company. Those insurance guys always give me a pain. They act like I cause all these burns. Let's go down in the basement and look around at what's left of the garage."

Tom Delaney coughed as smoke stung his throat.

"I thought it looked as though it started on the main floor," he objected. "How could flame get through this concrete?"

"Elevator shafts," said Blackford. "It always looks as though it started on the main floor. That's because fire burns upward."

"Sounds reasonable, but I think I'll look around up here."

"Go ahead," said Blackford, amiably, and followed the detective over to the front wall.

Tom Delaney broke out his own flashlight and stabbed it through the foggy interior, probing into piles of goods and along the floor. He went slowly ahead, marveling that anyone could ever trace arson in such a hideous shambles.

Then he stopped with something like a shudder and played the light on a charred hand which jutted out from beneath a counter. He bent down and then straightened up.

"I'll send in the morgue wagon when we go outside. That's one of your missing girls, Blackford."

Blackford looked quickly away. "I found the other two."

"Uh-huh. Both dead, weren't they? This isn't only arson, it's first-degree murder. That is, if the fire was more than an accident. Funny they couldn't have seen the flames coming at them."

"Panic," muttered the investigator. "People get trampled."

"Sure, but it was almost closing time when this fire started, and there couldn't have been many in the building. I think we'll find that it started on this floor, and in more than one place."

Blackford sighed. "It takes a detective to figure all that out. I wouldn't have thought about it, I guess."

Tom Delaney said nothing more. He walked ahead still

lashing the counters with his light. This must have been the dress goods department, he judged. Then once more he stopped and stood looking down. Blackford came up and peered over the detective's shoulder.

"Bottle glass," said Delaney. "Now what the devil could bottle glass be doing here?"

Blackford shrugged and picked a fragment up, sniffing at it.

"Furniture polish. They used it to polish the counters, I guess."

But the detective took the fire-dulled splinter from the investigator and shoved it into his pocket.

"Maybe so, but I'll analyze this for explosive or acid. Nothing like being thorough."

He began to search the floor over a radius of fifteen feet. Painstakingly he went over the charred and littered surface, moving unrecognizable objects, examining others. And then he found a piece of copper wire. Slowly he traced it down and uncovered another thread of metal.

"Does insulation burn off extension cords?" he asked.

"Sometimes."

"But if these things had had insulation on them, there'd be charred pieces. And"—he reached down and scooped up a bit of straw—"excelsior."

Blackford smiled tolerantly. "They pack a lot of things in excelsior in department stores. Come on, I've got to get busy. We have a certain routine that usually gives us the answer, and I'll have to have a report in another hour. I'm going outside and get another battery for my light. This thing is getting pretty dim."

Delaney nodded. "I'll go with you."

They worked through the choking fog to the door, skirting the ruins in the aisles and carefully avoiding the spot where the dead girl lay.

When they stepped into the open air, Delaney took a long, deep, grateful breath.

"I'll get the morgue squad," he said, "and then go up to Headquarters and analyze this glass." Idly he watched a black sedan draw up to the curb not ten feet away.

"Okay," said Blackford. "If you find anything—"

A pistol shot, as vicious as it was unexpected, gouged the concrete near Delaney's feet. A harsh, strident voice bellowed:

"Up with the mitts, you guys, or we'll let you have it."

Delaney started to reach for his own gun and then realized that he was checkmated. Slowly he elevated his hands and watched two men walk toward him through the thin stream of light from the street lamp.

"Connely," grunted the detective. "And Soapy Jackson."

"Know us, do you?" grated Connely. "Seen us in the lineup, that it? Turn around, both of you!"

Delaney turned because he knew that this pair always meant what they said. He saw Soapy Jackson bring a blackjack down on Blackford's head—and then something crashed against his own skull. He stumbled bitterly forward into unconsciousness.

CHAPTER TWO

READY FOR ROASTING

THEY could not have gone far, for the car was stopped when Detective-Sergeant Tom Delaney regained his battered senses. He sat up and found that a pistol muzzle was prodding him in the side.

"Git along, little cop," said Soapy Jackson. "Walk up those steps and don't look back. We'll be right behind you."

Staggering slightly, Delaney climbed down from the car, discovering that his hands were tied behind his back. His topcoat was dusty and his hat had been lost, allowing his dark hair to cascade down over his face. He shook it out of his eyes and went up the steps, feeling helpless and weak.

"Y'don't like to be sapped, hey?" said Connely. "Serves you right, flatfoot."

Soapy Jackson kicked open a door and for the first time Delaney took account of his surroundings. This house was neither old nor shabby. It was bounded by a beautiful landscaped yard which showed care even in the dim light of evening. The knocker on the door was brightly polished. But, evidently, there were no occupants, for Jackson stamped through the halls as though he owned the entire building.

Standing beside the door he had thrown open, Connely pointed into a dark closet.

"This is good enough," he said. "Throw him in."

Delaney was knocked off balance by a shove against his shoulder. Head first, unable to catch himself, he pitched into the cramped interior. Jackson kicked his legs out of the doorway.

"Listen, flatfoot," said Connely. "Just for your peace of mind, listen for the doorbell. When it rings, that'll be the signal for you to start practicing on a harp."

"If they give dead cops harps," added Jackson, chuckling. "But even if you do get one, you're going to get a little taste of hell first."

He shoved a dirty handkerchief into Delaney's mouth and tied it there with another. That done, he slammed and locked the door, leaving the detective in darkness blacker than ink.

For the next five minutes, Delaney lay still, listening and marshaling his swimming senses. He heard the two mobsters pounding around the first floor and heard their muffled voices calling to each other across the length of the empty house.

Evidently they were not worried about interference. And then the front door slammed and the building was as silent as it was dark.

Delaney tried vainly to put the jigsaw puzzle together. He knew that detectives were often rubbed out for no apparent reason other than vengeance, but he did not understand just why he had been picked up at Tyler's Department Store. Too, Connely had said something about the doorbell, meaning, apparently, that other persons would enter and finish the work the mobsters had begun.

If he could only get out, Delaney knew exactly where to find Soapy Jackson and Connely. Like most gangsters, they had a common stomping ground where they could establish plenty of alibis. Even if anyone had seen them strike the detective and Blackford down, the assailants could prove that they were not involved in the killing of the detective—for the coroner would be unable to establish exactly the length of time Delaney had been dead.

The worst that could happen to Connely and Jackson would be accessory to the fact—a charge easily shed with the aid of a smart lawyer.

For a few moments Delaney wondered what had happened to Blackford, and then decided that the investigator had not been wanted. The mobsters were looking for revenge, that was all. Perhaps one of their friends had been sent up through Delaney's efforts. Delaney tried to remember and then gave it up.

He was feeling considerably better physically and considerably worse mentally when he discovered that his feet were not tied. He moved them restlessly and kicked at the door, without result.

And then he remembered that Blaze Delaney, the fire-eater, was slated for the retirement list and disgrace, and the fact did something to him. It would break the old man's heart to be ousted just because he didn't have enough equipment to fight the flames which were gradually reducing the city to charred embers—and just that would happen if the present rate of fires kept up. Tom Delaney must do something.

He reared back on his knees, bracing his shoulder against the wall. Slowly and carefully he worked himself up to his feet and stood, tottering. Experimentally, he slammed his shoulder against the door and found that the unnatural position of his hands made the impact extremely painful against his shoulder. Nevertheless, he heaved himself against the door once more.

Just as he braced himself for a third try against the stubborn wood, he heard the doorbell ring. The sound of its jangling made a shiver course its way down his spine. It seemed to have a significance other than the arrival of more gangsters.

Close on the heels of the bell came a sullen throb, not unlike the heavy jar of a falling wall. Delaney stiffened, waiting for the sound of footsteps, but none came. The house was tomblike in its silence.

But not for long. A thin, reedy crackle whispered through the keyhole of the locked closet door and grew steadily in volume. Suddenly Delaney's nostrils quivered with the harsh odor of smoke. The house was burning!

Something like panic welled up in Delaney's chest. He had faced guns and fists and unknown deaths, but the knowledge that he was about to be burned alive made all other dangers seem small. He set his teeth and hurled himself against the heavy door, a hiss escaping his teeth as the impact sent hot agony down his arm.

He turned his other side to the panels and crashed with renewed force. Above the growing roar of flames, he thought he heard the wood splinter. Summoning all the strength in his body, the detective sent himself forward like a hurtling projectile.

The door shivered away from its mooring and crashed forward, Delaney toppling on its surface. All air had been hammered out of him, but he checked himself from taking a deep breath. Smoke hung about his face though he was in its thinnest strata—the floor. For an instant he marveled at the rapidity with which the fire had spread.

He struggled upward until his face was three feet from the floor. There he knew he would find the cleanest air and an absence of the heavy, poisonous gases which mushroomed against the planks under his knees. He was "breathing from the top," for he knew that unconsciousness would come if he dragged deeply at the hot, acrid air.

Moving forward on his knees, he fought his way to the front door. He tried to stand up to turn the knob, but it was locked from the outside. For an instant he pressed his face to a crack and breathed clean air. The gag and the smoke were doing their best to choke him.

From there, he struggled along the wall toward another doorway which loomed dimly through the gray mist. The heat was shriveling, but Delaney went on, tripping, trying to see out of smarting eyes. At last he was through the portal, but the fire was licking through the wall at the other end of the room.

He felt his eyebrows and hair grow crisp and singed. He swore into the gag and tried to find a window.

At last a cool pane of glass touched his face and he drew back thankfully. With great difficulty he climbed up on the sill and kicked savagely. Glass showered to the floor, and the outrushing blast of heated air took Delaney with it.

CHAPTER THREE

TALKING BUSINESS

WITHOUT knowing just how he came to be there, he sat up on the lawn and looked at the burning structure, which now was sending showers of sparks and geysers of flames into the black night. Smoke rolled starward and mushroomed down like some evil bird of prey.

Delaney got to his feet and walked as rapidly as possible toward the sidewalk, watching the gathering crowd for a bluecoat. Someone opened the gate for him and then a policeman materialized with an amazed gasp.

"Delaney! What the devil are you—" And then he saw the gag and quickly removed it. From his pocket he whipped a knife with which he cut the rope that held the detective's hands.

"Thanks, Terrill," said Delaney, moving his sore mouth as little as possible. "Did you turn in an alarm?"

"Sure I did, but I haven't seen nothin' of the outfit yet."

"Probably busy at two or three other fires. Where's your patrol car?"

Terrill pointed to the machine and elbowed a way for the detective. People jamming the sidewalk shook their heads and murmured sullenly about the laxity of the fire department. Delaney gave no sign that he heard, his mind too busy with the project at hand. He slid under the wheel.

"I'll send this back from Headquarters," he said. "Stand by

for the fire engines." He pulled the whistle cord wide open and went hurtling away through the traffic.

Blaze Delaney was not the only one who prided himself on being able to put a car through the streets in a hurry. He had passed the ability on to his son. Within five minutes, the detective braked in front of Headquarters and leaped out, sprinting up the three floors to the squad room.

His inspector gasped across his desk through the open door.

"Delaney! What on earth have you been into? You look like a cinder."

"I feel like one," said the detective. "I lost my gun. Got one handy?"

"You're in a devil of a hurry." He fished a revolver out of a cluttery drawer and pushed it across into Delaney's hands. "You better clean up before you go out. That's a helluva way to go off duty."

"I'm not going off duty," Delaney shot over his shoulder. "And I'll look worse in no time at all." He leaned over the railing and barked at the desk sergeant: "Where can I find my dad?"

"Dunno," said the sergeant ponderously. "There's three unattended fires waiting for him right now, and I don't know which he'll hit first. But I ain't supposed to know."

Delaney soared down the flights of steps, pausing only long enough to detail a man to return Terrill's car. He found his own machine at the curb and climbed aboard. The exhaust whistle chortled insanely and the car swerved headlong into a cluster of taxis which parted like frightened chickens.

But the detective cut down his speed and shut off the racket two blocks away from his destination. As softly and silently as a ghost, he drifted into a parking place opposite a pool hall he knew very well.

He sat for an instant getting his breath before he climbed down, looking up at the red glows which spotted the sky. At no time in its history had the city seen so many fires burning at the same time. The newspapers had exhausted themselves sending out extras. Delaney saw a paper now in the hand of a howling boy. He received a glimpse of the headlines.

Mayor to Oust Delaney!
NEGLIGENCE—

So they were going to put the skids under his dad after all, in spite of anything Blaze Delaney could do. Right now the chief of fire-eaters was out fighting the battle of his life against flame, and up in the city hall—or more likely in a comfortable sitting room, this time of night—the mayor was denouncing and forgetting that he had cut down the fire department himself in the name of economy.

But the detective had too many things on his mind to worry long about mere mayors. He got out of his car and walked slowly and purposefully in the direction of the lighted entrance.

From within came the sounds of clicking balls and arguing men. An electric piano poured out its strident heart in an attempt to drown conversation. An electric sign advertised "Joe's Social Hall. Beer. Snooker Pool."

Delaney pushed back both swinging doors at once and

stepped through into the yellow lights. The bartender glanced up from a dice game, surprise making his face flabby.

"What's the matter, Delaney?" croaked the loose throat.

But the detective was not there to waste talk. He stalked along the length of the bottle-flanked mirrors until he saw his quarry.

Soapy Jackson and Connely were leaning over cues. They were without their coats and the caliber of the place was clearly emphasized by the fact that both mobsters exhibited shoulder holsters in plain sight.

Connely's chin went in with a jerk and he blinked his black beady eyes. He touched Jackson's shoulder.

"Pipe the dick."

Evenly, as though motivated by a slow-motion mechanism, Jackson turned. But Jackson's nerves were not as good as Connely's. His hands started to shake and he dropped his cue with a startled "Gosh! Delaney!"

The detective's hand was suddenly shadowed by a revolver.

"I want you two birds," he snapped. "Get your coats."

But the two gangsters were not without friends. Before they could move, a pistol butt and face jutted up over Delaney's shoulder and the butt started down. Jackson's eyes narrowed instinctively and the detective understood with a practice born of a thousand such situations. He dived sideways and his gun roared. The puffy-faced wielder of the weapon swore luridly and grabbed at his blood-spurting wrist.

Connely's hand shot to his shoulder holster and came out spitting. His gun belched flame a second time before Delaney's bullet sent him thudding back against the wall.

The detective's hand was suddenly shadowed by a revolver.
"I want you two birds," he snapped.

Jackson stood shaking, glancing to left and right, looking for an out.

And then Delaney's singed, calm face came up through a ring of powder smoke.

"I usually mean what I say," he rapped. "Walk right ahead of me, quick, and never mind those coats. You won't need 'em where you're going."

Jackson and Connely walked stiffly, the latter holding his shoulder and moaning. The bartender tried to catch Delaney's attention and apologize, but the detective walked out through the doors unheeding.

At the car, the detective removed an oddly limp blackjack from Jackson, pulled two pairs of handcuffs out of the side pocket and snapped them on docilely offered wrists.

"Listen," whined Jackson. "Can't we talk business on this thing?"

"No. Get in."

The two slumped into the seat, looking helplessly about, shivering slightly as the night breeze cut through their shirt sleeves. While Delaney was starting the car, Jackson spoke again.

"Listen. I got ten grand in a safe-deposit box—"

"Shut up!" rasped Connely. "He'll get us for bribery! Ain't you got any sense?"

Delaney drove the car for several blocks before the two noticed that they weren't heading for the police station.

"Listen," said Connely, "I gotta get this shoulder fixed. I'll bleed to death."

"Go ahead," Delaney snapped. "It'll save the state the price of electricity."

"Aw, have a heart, copper. We didn't mean no harm." Connely stopped long enough to emit a heart-rending moan.

"I'm going to take you birds with me," said the detective. "I've got a little research to do, and after that we'll go back to the station house and try out the rubber hose on you. I've got an idea that it'll work."

Jackson grunted dolefully.

"You don't have to do that, copper. We'll spill right now if you want us to."

"Go ahead."

"If we turn state's evidence, will you let us off?" demanded Connely, miraculously reviving.

"I'm not promising you birds anything. I don't have to have your dope. I've got just about all I need right now. The big boy talked plenty fast."

"You mean—" began Jackson.

"Shut up," hissed Connely. "He's baiting us."

Jackson's mouth took on a traplike aspect. Jammed as he was between the wounded Connely and the unmoved Delaney, he cautiously tried to find out how close he could come to wrecking the car. But Delaney's hands were steel clamps on the spokes.

"Scared, aren't you?" said Delaney evenly. "All I can say is, you'll be a whole lot more scared in a couple hours."

Ahead, the gutted ruins of Tyler's Department Store loomed. Several bluecoats were posted there now, keeping out any possible looters who might try to get away with charred valuables. Smoke still hung about the structure like a dreary cloak.

The detective drew up to the curb and called to an officer to keep an eye on the two occupants of the roadster. Borrowing a flashlight, he went into the building and stayed for several minutes. Presently he came out and climbed in under the wheel.

"Need any help?" queried the policeman.

"No, thanks," said Delaney. "You got any idea where I can find Blaze Delaney?"

"Huh! He's all over the city tonight. I heard there were sixteen fires going at the same time." The officer stepped back and thought for a moment. "I can call the fire department for you."

"Go ahead," said Delaney.

In a few seconds, the policeman was back. "He's working at Sixteenth and Bushman, according to the latest. It was seventeen fires instead of sixteen. I hear they're going to throw old man Delaney out on his ear. That right?"

The detective shook his head.

"Just rumor. My dad's in there to stay."

"Glad to hear it." The policeman smiled after the accelerating machine.

The passage between Tyler's and Sixteenth and Bushman streets was made in record time, with the squad car chortling like a mad banshee. Ahead the sky was growing redder and smokier, until Delaney could smell the fire itself. It was not hard to smell smoke on this night. Spots in the overcast heavens hung like red ulcers above the town.

At the edge of the fire lines, Delaney spotted the red coupe and drove in as close as he could. Two policemen were vainly striving to keep the street clear for the smoke-eaters.

"Dobson!" shouted Delaney, and waited until Officer Dobson came. "Look after these two mugs, will you? I've got some business. Where's Blaze Delaney?"

Dobson gestured with his thumb and leaned against the running board, thankful for a chance to rest.

The detective was not long in spotting the chief of the fire department. Blaze Delaney stood with his feet wide apart, bullying tired firemen to greater effort and directing the hard campaign against this particular two-story structure. He saw his son and his reddened eyes asked a vital question.

"Not yet," said the detective. "Keep right on. You're pretty close to fighting your last fire tonight." He smiled and cast about, attempting to recognize another individual. Finally he spotted Blackford and went up to him.

The investigator was standing on the outskirts of the fighters, looking on, a little bored. When he saw the detective he blinked and his thin face twitched.

"Hello," he greeted. "Glad to see you got out of it all right." He pointed to a bandage around his forehead. "They didn't take me with them."

"No," said Delaney. "I don't guess they did. I found this on Jackson." He extracted a limp black thing from his pocket and patted it against the palm of his hand.

"Huh! I've seen plenty of blackjacks," grunted Blackford.

"Not like this, you haven't." Delaney held it up. "It's stuffed with cotton batting."

"Well, that's funny."

"Funny as a morgue," snapped Delaney. "You haven't got so much as a bump on your head. When Soapy Jackson sapped you with a cotton blackjack, you fell down and played possum to make it look good. Furthermore, your pals have been babbling their heads off."

Blackford's face was frozen in stunned surprise. All his nonchalance slid away from him like an avalanche. In the jumpy firelight his skin was ashen.

"They—they talked? You mean—"

Delaney smiled twistedly and knew he had scored.

"Look out there at that squad car," he snapped.

The investigator looked, and if he had been disconcerted before, he was wild with terror now. His eyes went wider and his jaw slacked, showing unclean teeth. Something like a strangled sob came up in his throat.

And then it was as though his entire nervous system had snapped. He was hemmed in on all sides save one. Policemen and firemen stood to either side and in back of him. The only cleared ground lay between the lines and the fire. Blackford choked again, his eyes holding an insane light.

And then, before the weary Delaney could understand what had happened, he saw with a violent shock that Blackford had started to sprint straight toward the flames. Whether it was an attempt at suicide or a crazed blindness, Delaney did not stop to reason. Like a catapulted projectile, he was off in pursuit.

CHAPTER FOUR

THE FAMILY PRESTIGE

THE fire was beating hotly against the detective's face, but he plowed ahead. Behind him Blaze Delaney was running and shouting. A fireman tried to catch the detective's billowing topcoat. But Blackford was already disappearing through the smoke-filled doorway of the crackling structure. Delaney saw it with a sinking heart, knowing that Blackford was determined not to be taken alive.

But the detective's case was not closed. There were many loose ends he could never hope to patch without Blackford's confession. He plunged into the welter of gray geysering smoke, forgetful in his zeal that he himself might be engulfed and killed.

Inside there was neither visibility nor air. The instant the lighted patch which was the door behind him disappeared, Delaney knew that he was lost in appallingly close confines. He was immediately deserted by his sense of direction, for in stumbling through the blinding haze he could not walk in a straight line.

He collided with harshly solid objects, tripping and lunging forward, groping for a wall, trying to keep his face three feet above the floor in the air strata. And then he fell over a soft object which lay inert. It was Blackford.

The last thing Delaney remembered was pulling Blackford

away and trying to locate the entrance. The smoke tore at his lungs and the gray fog went black. He fell unconscious across the investigator.

And then the detective was trying to sit up and someone was gently holding him back. He tried several times before he experimentally opened his eyes. He sighed with relief, for he was looking into the face of a worried Blaze Delaney.

"Lay still, blast it!" said the chief. "You had me worried for a while, and if you don't stay still you'll have me worried again."

"You pulled me out?" croaked the detective.

"Sure. It wasn't any trick with a gas mask. What was the idea of chasing Blackford into that place, and why the devil was Blackford trying to commit suicide?"

"Blackford's the firebug," said the detective, coughing.

"Go on! You're smoke-dippy."

The detective shook his head. "I'm not. How long has Blackford been in your department?"

"Why, let's see," pondered Blaze Delaney. "About a year. He came here from the Chicago department with some fine letters of recommendation."

And then Delaney the younger lurched to his feet and kicked the stretcher away from him. There was no holding him down, even though the old fire-eater tried hard.

Blackford was lying in a wire basket beside an ambulance and the smoke-grimed attendant beside him was administering oxygen.

"He's coming around," said the intern. "That was close."

The detective gave vent to a hacking cough which was immediately stilled when he saw Blackford's eyes spring open.

"Hello, alias Blackford," said Delaney, kneeling down on the pavement beside the man.

The investigator shut his eyes tightly and groaned.

"Snap out of it," said the detective. "You're going to do some talking right here and now. What did you do with the original Blackford?"

"I'm him," whined the investigator with a beseeching look at the chief of fire-eaters.

Tom Delaney looked up with a slow wink as though to inform Blaze Delaney that this game was being played in the dark.

"Yeah?" said Delaney the younger. "I happen to know you murdered him and took his papers before he had a chance to contact the department here. And you might as well not try to deny it!" He snatched at the dirty coat front and lifted alias Blackford up, shaking him. "Talk or I'll pound you into hamburger!"

Fear widened the investigator's eyes as he saw the hard, set jaw. His mouth twitched and he tried to swallow.

Delaney shook him again and raised a knotted fist.

"That's right," croaked the investigator, quickly.

"That's better," rapped Delaney the younger. "Who paid you to make these phony reports and overlook fires that had been set?"

"Nobody," whined "Blackford." "We got hold of owners that needed the insurance money and split with them."

"I thought so. And your favorite trick was taking a bottle of nitroglycerin, wrapping it in excelsior and putting electric wires over the mouth. That right?"

When the other had nodded weakly, the detective went on: "And you hooked the electric wires to doorbells so that the fires never started until your pair of henchmen were miles away with a good alibi. You started the Tyler Department Store fire by connecting several 'soup' bottles to the light switch which you knew would be turned on just before closing."

Dismally, alias Blackford nodded assent. His was the expression of a thoroughly whipped dog.

"Well," continued Delaney, standing up, "you'll face murder on a dozen different counts, and arson. You and your pals out there in the squad car will certainly get mighty burnt. Did you set any more fires for tonight?"

"No," whimpered the investigator. "Don't I get anything off for turning state's evidence?"

"You didn't have to talk," snapped Delaney, "but I've a dozen witnesses that you did. It'll take more than a smart mouthpiece to clear you of this rap. And furthermore, you're going to turn over a list of every man who allowed you to work on his property. Understand?"

Alias Blackford understood. He lay like a sack of soggy straw and nodded only with an effort. Dully he watched the two Delaneys move away.

"But how . . . how," began the old fire-eater, "how did you ever get next to all this? You're leaving a lot of it out. I've done some detecting in my time, but I never grabbed clues out of thin air that way."

"Thin air," grinned the detective. "No thin air about that. I had to take some awful beatings to get that dope. Don't I look like it?"

"You sure do," affirmed the elder Delaney, gruffly. "What happened to you?"

"They caught me at the Tyler store when I came out with Blackford. Smashed me on the head with a sap, carried me off and set a fire under me. They thought I knew a lot more than I did. Blackford thought I was wise when he first laid eyes on me. He tipped off his boys to be on the alert and then when I found some bottle glass inside—"

"Bottle glass?"

"Sure. I was going to take it up to the laboratory for analysis just on a hunch. And Blackford knew that I'd find a trace of nitroglycerin on that fragment. And when I did, I'd be sure the fire was of incendiary origin. He was scared, and when we came out he signaled his boys to jump me.

"They tied me up in a closet and wired a bottle of 'soup' to the doorbell. Then they went out and established an alibi and sent a messenger boy back to the house to ring the bell. He rang it and blowie! The place was on fire."

"Nitroglycerin set off by electricity," growled the fire-eater. "What the devil will pyromaniacs think up next? You were mighty lucky to get out, Son. It looks like those fellows meant business."

"I'll say they did. They weren't going to have their game queered if they could help it. You see, Blackford made that snatch look good by having himself knocked out, supposedly. I found a cotton blackjack on one of his boys. If it hadn't been for the blackjack and that piece of glass, we'd still be fighting fires all over the town."

"And thanks to you, we aren't," said old Delaney with more

than a hint of pride. He pulled at his mustache and then looked up to see an acquaintance coming toward him. "Hello, Morley."

Morley of Graysons' Insurance came up beside them.

"So you're the fair-haired lad that cleared up this mess." He touched the detective's shoulder. "Is it against your code to accept rewards?"

"Well," hesitated the younger Delaney, "we don't usually—Wait a minute. You need some new carts and hose, don't you, Dad?"

"Gosh, yes. They got me cut to the bone."

"Fine," said the detective. "Hear that? Tell your company to make out the reward as a donation to the fire department. They shouldn't be very slow in doing that."

"I'll say not," replied the insurance agent. "You've saved us something like a million dollars in claims, maybe more. I don't think Graysons' will forget it very fast. In fact, we'd like to get you appointed in Blackford's place. We've got the influence, you know."

"Huh," grunted the fire-eater. "That isn't such a bad idea. Better pay and shorter hours. What about it, Son?"

"Not bad. Maybe I could keep you out of hot water. An hour ago, extras were on the streets saying that you were going to be kicked out. Hurts the family prestige, things like that. I guess I'd better take the job." The detective grinned.

"I always said I'd make a fireman out of you," growled Blaze Delaney, and then fell to tugging fiercely at his mustache to hide the pleasure in his smoke-stung eyes.

CALLING SQUAD CARS!

CALLING SQUAD CARS!

JIM COLLINS lowered his troubled head and hunched his broad, capable shoulders against the rain. Idly he kicked at a paper which lay in his path on the sidewalk and then, as his foot opened a soggy page, he stared ruefully at the headlines which greeted his eye.

POLICE DISCOVER NEW LEAD IN HUNT FOR "ONE-EYE" TASCORI MOB.

POLICE RADIO ANNOUNCER COLLINS DISCHARGED FROM HEADQUARTERS AS INSPECTOR GRIFFITH LINKS HIM WITH EVASIVE MARAUDERS.

Jim Collins, police radio announcer, was released on bail tonight as net tightens in the search for the mob of "One-Eye" Tascori whose citywide robberies and depredations have amazed and shocked citizens.

There was more to it. A great deal more. It covered part of the front and slithered over to the second page in a slimy trail of water-soaked ink. Collins kicked at it once more and then resumed his aimless wandering.

For weeks an ugly cloud of suspicion had hovered over his brown head. For days his soft southern voice had borne a slight edge of worry, and then, tonight, the blow had fallen.

Collins had been seated behind his mike in the control room utilizing an idle moment to drive home the last plate in the miniature microphones he was perfecting. Through his mind had run the endless chain of remarks which had drummed in upon him. Neither detectives nor policemen had spoken to him kindly for days.

The chief had appeared beside the control board. Glaring down at Collins, he had said, "The jig's up, sonny. You're under arrest!"

They had led him back to the dreaded degree rooms at the rear of the building. They had placed him in a hard chair, turned a brilliant light on his face, to begin their endless chain of questioning.

Collins had shaken his head dazedly. "I can't explain why calls go out which never appear on my record. I can't explain why a voice like mine calls squad cars away from the scene of Tascori's crimes. I don't know, I swear I don't know!" His usually soft voice mounted slightly in his earnestness.

The chief had clicked his teeth together, his jaw close to Collins' face.

"Listen, Collins, every time 'One-Eye' Tascori has robbed a bank or stuck up a speakeasy, you've been at the mike. And every time the cars have suddenly been called away from the scene of the robbery to attend a fire which wasn't burning, to rescue a drowning man who didn't exist.

"I know that you use that police radio to help Tascori, so come clean. Where does he hang out? What is the name of his gang?"

For hours the inquisition had gone on but young Collins,

worn and haggard by the unceasing fire of the chief's snarling voice, had been adamant in his protest of his innocence.

Finally the chief had given up with the threat that Collins would cool his heels in jail until he cared to divulge the information. But the chief had been thwarted in that for McCarty, the other announcer, had gone his bail.

Now he was on the loose. His job was gone. His reputation was ruined. Newspaper headlines screamed at him from the racks along the sidewalk. With a meager final paycheck in his pocket he faced imminent poverty, perhaps starvation, for although he was a crack radioman, firms would hardly hire one who dwelled under a constant cloud of suspicion.

Ahead of him, Collins could see the light of a doorway below the street. He knew the place well. It was a speakeasy of considerable size. He examined the contents of his pockets with damp fingers.

The two miniature microphones he had taken from his desk clanked together lonesomely. Aside from that small check, he was broke. But he shrugged his shoulders and headed for the doorway. Though he rarely drank, he felt the need of a stimulant now. Perhaps it would aid his buzzing head.

At the head of the stairs, the crash of a pistol met him from below. Rapidly it was followed by two others. A scream and a babble of voices burst through the suddenly opened door as four men jumped up the stairs. They brushed Collins aside roughly and ran for a car which waited at the curb with running motor. But Collins had seen just enough. The man in the lead had only one eye!

The radioman's eyes went blank for an instant as he

remembered newspaper pictures of Tascori. Then, with a leap, he was to the curb, unseen by the hastily embarking men. Collins jumped into a ring of tires on the back of the car and the machine sped away through the rain.

Collins puckered his mouth. Now that he was this far, where did he go from here? Quickly he tried to fit a plan together. The machine's rubber tires were whining over the pavement as it sped southward through the city.

Coming darkness and the increasing rain hid him from the eyes of the traffic police, but he dared not signal as the car passed directed intersections lest the men ahead might notice.

It suddenly came to him that he was weaponless, save for his two fists and his wits. Where the car was going he did not know, nor did he know his course of action when it arrived. He could only crouch in the darkness and await his chance.

There were five in the car, counting the driver. Five men who had just committed the most heinous of crimes, murder for robbery. They were the most dangerous men in the underworld, daring everything and anything. They had indirectly ruined the radioman, and so he clung to the tires and gritted his teeth against the ache which was seeping up his taut muscles.

Collins hunched down and tried to map out some plan. What if he were spotted when the men stopped the car? What if they halted at some well-lighted filling station? What if the car blew a tire? He held himself in readiness with aching arms and waited, his eyes narrow as vivid bits of this chain of events passed through his mind.

Well in the outskirts of the city, on an unlighted street, the car stopped in the driveway of a huge unlighted house which loomed dark and forbidding in the rain. Holding his breath lest a light suddenly betray him, Collins stepped gingerly away from the car and slid under a dripping bush. The headlights had been switched off at the moment of arrival, but through the rain-soaked blackness, the radioman caught the movement of figures mounting the steps to the building. Wet leather crunched against stone and gravel.

An ugly voice said, "Take the bus around back, Tony, and gas her up. Look over the motor, check the tires, and see you don't let her fall down on us! Get going!"

The car slid back to the street and headed for an alleyway. By the light of his lamps, Collins saw four men trudge up to the high doorway. He stiffened as he glimpsed again the black patch which hid Tascori's sightless socket.

The door slammed, and with rain trickling down inside his light topcoat, Collins crept to the side of the house. Looking up he saw a crack of light on the first floor. A light flickered through the blinds of another window.

Decisively, the radioman returned to the front. With wet hands he examined the pillars which supported the porch roof. With a grain of luck he saw that he could climb them noiselessly and swing himself to the top of the porch roof with the aid of a lattice.

Carefully he mounted the railing and reached up. He swung his legs around the post and began the ascent. It was tedious, difficult work, for his arms were tired from the long strain of hanging to the back of the car.

Cautiously he felt for the latticework, grasped the thin slats with a silent prayer that they would support his weight, and heaved his long body up and out.

Doubling suddenly, he projected himself onto the roof. Hanging with his head down he felt along the slippery shingles for holds, found them and drew himself toward the white frame of a window which gleamed dully in the blackness.

He felt in his pockets for a knife, disentangled the clasp from several coils of thin wire which he had absently picked up from his worktable at headquarters, and inserted the blade under the sill.

Slowly, lest he snap the thin blade, he pulled up. With a sigh, the window opened. The dank smell of a cold, damp room greeted his nostrils and he placed his dripping legs over the sill.

He rested his weight on one foot and tested the boards around him. Finding that none of them creaked, Collins turned and closed down the window.

At last he was inside the house, a floor above Tascori. Unarmed, yes, but confidence swarmed in upon him as he realized that luck, so far, had been with him.

At the door of the room, he pressed his ear to a crack and listened. Far below him he could hear the murmur of men's voices. Silently, Collins opened the door and cast his eyes over the hall which lay before him. At his right, a stairway led down, allowing some of the light from below to flicker on the walls.

The sound of voices had grown louder and Collins knew that Tascori was in the room at the bottom of those stairs.

Tensely he waited for all of the men to take their turn at talking.

One, two, three, and then the harsh, ugly rasp of Tascori as he derided one of the men for a clumsy piece of work.

A chair creaked and one of the men started across the room, his voice growing louder in the radioman's ears.

Suddenly something told Collins that the man was about to ascend the stairs and he glanced up to see if a light lay above him. But the house was too old to have such a thing as remote light control, and Collins breathed deeply.

The man's feet were stomping on the boards. He had ceased to talk.

Knowing that inky blackness lay behind him, and that the gangster's eyes were accustomed to the bright light of the room below, Collins glanced around the corner. In his belt the other carried a heavy automatic.

Excitement tugged at the radioman's heart, causing it to beat out of time. All the bitterness which he had borne suddenly leaped up and became strength. His strong, dark face tensed. He felt the blood throbbing in his temples until he was almost certain that the other could hear the rapid hammering of his heart. Wages of failure here would be a quick death.

The gangster reached the last step below the upper landing but a few inches away from Collins. With a lunge, the radioman snatched out and grasped the butt of that gun. It came free with a wrench.

Surprised, the other grunted and stepped back, tottering on the stairs.

Collins smashed the pistol into his startled face with such force that the gangster plunged backwards, left the stairs and with a long crash hurtled toward the bottom.

Collins plunged after him three steps at a time. A moment's hesitation would cost him his victory. Almost as the other hit the first floor, Collins was beside him.

"Freeze!" he shouted to the others. "Grab for the ceiling!" He thrust the gun out as though the very force of it would hold the others motionless.

Tascori spat like a caged tiger. His two henchmen remained where they were and slowly raised their arms upward. Caught sitting down and with only an instant's warning, they were helpless.

"Stand up!" cried Collins. He motioned with the gun. "Stand up and turn your faces to that wall!"

Tascori's one eye kindled and darted to a door which was now behind the radioman's back. He stiffened and then slumped wearily. For an instant a crafty light had gleamed darkly in that one orb, but flushed with excitement and the elation of victory, Collins had not noticed.

The three, hampered by their upraised arms, climbed to their feet. Sullenness and despair marked each face. In fact, their sudden expressions of dejection were so complete and spontaneous that the radioman might have been warned. Following Tascori's meek example, the other two turned and faced the indicated wall.

Collins, with a glance into the automatic's breech to make sure that it held a cartridge, strode forward. A bulge in Tascori's hip pocket caught his eye. With intent to disarm the gangster, the radioman reached out. It had been too easy! A smile played over his face.

He had just touched the bulge when the room seemed to split apart with a roar. The wall and men spun before his eyes. A mighty hand was dragging him to the floor, relentless, dark, awful. Suddenly he stopped fighting against the force. He had never been so terribly tired in his life. Everything gave a final spin and vanished in blackness.

Tascori leered down at the motionless figure. "Nice work, Tony," he said tonelessly to the newcomer who stood in the door by the stairs, holding a smoking pistol.

The one-eyed man was tall and gaunt with a pinched face and narrow, cruel lips. The black patch over the empty socket stood out starkly against the yellow pallor of his skin. He stooped down over the body and examined the wound in Collins' head. The man called Tony stepped to his side.

Tascori jerked up with an explosive oath. "Bungler! You've just creased him!"

"I'm sorry," said Tony, stepping back. "I shot in such a hurry." He shrugged his shoulders and fingered his automatic. Then an idea mirrored itself on his face. "But that's easy to fix up." He looked down at the sprawled body of the radioman. "That's easy."

Without hesitating he kneeled beside Collins and pressed the still-smoking muzzle of the pistol against the radioman's temple. Tascori grinned mirthlessly and said, "Go ahead."

Tony adjusted the muzzle carefully and squeezed the butt safety into place. His finger started to close down on the trigger. His face was expressionless. Then he drew the gun away and grasped Collins by the hair, turning his head over so that light fell on the unconscious features.

He glanced up at Tascori. "I think I'll do it this way this time. It's more sure." He laid a piece of newspaper under the brown hair. "No use messing up the rug much more."

Again he placed the pistol against Collins' head, but this time, its black muzzle was held under the throat. His palm came down on the butt safety again and his finger tightened against the trigger.

"Wait a minute!" blurted one of the men. "I know that guy!"

Tascori turned languidly. "Friend of yours?"

"No, I'll say not!" snapped the gangster. "He's the radio announcer at police headquarters! I saw him in the broadcasting room last time they dragged me into the bullpen."

"Are you sure?" demanded Tascori. He was staring down at Collins with new interest.

"Sure! You can look right through the glass as you come in the door to the desk." The gangster pointed down at the unconscious radioman with a bony finger. "I'd know him anyplace."

"Hm," muttered Tascori. "So this is our little friend the radio announcer we've been having so much fun with. Well, well, well. And we were going to bump him off just like that!"

He snapped his fingers and turned over the sprawling body with a disdainful foot.

"I'm sure that we can give him a much better time than that. Later this evening we'll take him for a nice little ride." He turned to the man who knew Collins. "Take that curtain and lash him into that chair."

The man whom Collins had sent hurtling down the steps lurched to his feet, pressing a hand against his bleeding nose. "I'll say we'll take him for a ride!" He planted a solid kick in the radioman's ribs.

Tascori had lost immediate interest in the proceedings. "Tony! Get out there and see if you can find something to eat. I'm hungry." He sat down in an upholstered chair and picked up a newspaper.

"Huh! No wonder he's here!" And he read the story which Collins had seen earlier in the evening. He glanced across the room to where two of his men were binding the radioman with strips torn from a cretonne curtain.

"Yes, you'll have a very enjoyable ride, I'm sure."

Collins awoke with the smell of cooking food in his nostrils. Pain shot through his skull as he moved, but he forced himself to lift his eyes so that he could stare about the room.

Suddenly the full portent of his presence clicked and he stiffened. When he tried to move his arms, he found that they were securely bound to the sides of the chair. He attempted to shift his legs, but they too were lashed down. He gazed for a long time at the ragged cretonne bonds, then he looked up and saw Tascori looking at him.

"Well," said Collins thickly, "I guess you win. What are you going to do with me?" Though his voice was hoarse, his southern drawl was apparent.

Tascori stretched out his legs and smiled crookedly at his captive. "I'm going to take you for a nice little ride, my boy."

Collins tautened and stared at the man. Those words had

been spoken with a lazy southern inflection, an exact imitation of his own drawling voice!

"Yes—a nice ride," Tascori laughed and fished a cigarette from his pocket. Lighting it, he tossed the burning match into the ashtray which stood at Collins' elbow, where it flickered fitfully among the heaped butts.

Tony thrust his head through the door. "Okay, Chief, the grub's on the table."

Tascori smiled at Collins for a moment, his one eye cold and narrow. "Won't you have something to eat with us? No?" He laughed and walked out of the room, leaving the radioman alone.

His headache had diminished somewhat and his mind was so filled with swift speculations that he forgot the clotted bullet crease above his ear. Tascori could imitate his voice! Perhaps—perhaps—

His eyes darted about the room and came to rest on two boxes which were set on a table against the wall. One he knew to be a small shortwave receiving set, very much like those which were placed in each of the squad cars.

The other was much larger. Its face was covered with meters and dials. An open switch stood beside the box. A complete radio broadcasting set of the latest compact type. Collins examined it narrowly. It was complete with the exception of the microphone. And the leads to that were coiled before it on the table top.

He suddenly realized the portent of his discovery. And a map of the city pinned above the radio broadcaster confirmed the matter. For that map had pins bearing numbers thrust into it. And the numbers corresponded to the squad cars, all in their proper districts.

It was plain now. Tascori's plan was simple. He would select the location of his next job, and garner the numbers of the police cars in that and surrounding districts.

He would pull the switch and give the official call in the exact imitation of Collins' voice. By tapping the shortwave receiver at the broadcaster, he would know when Collins would be at the police mike, and whether or not the police mike was silent.

Even if the police mike went to work in the middle of Tascori's call, he would know by the sudden crackle when to quit. After giving the call, he would race with his gang to the scene of his next crime, certain of being unmolested.

Collins was suddenly calm. A resolve stronger than he was throwing new strength into his battered muscles. Coldly his brain seized upon facts and methodically placed them together.

He looked down at his side and saw the slight bulge which the two tiny microphones made in his pocket. Earlier in the evening he had discovered that several coils of uncovered wire were in his coat pocket. And his coat lay beside him on the floor where the gangsters had thrown it.

If he could attach that mike— He wrenched at his bonds. Looking down again, he saw that they were of thin cloth. He tugged again. The cloth refused to give. Collins' heart began to sink and his resolve started to ebb.

The cloth was cretonne, almost impossible to tear. And its folds were wrapped so tightly that circulation was dead in his hands and feet. A sob of disappointment welled up in his throat. So near, yet so far, he was unable to reach that broadcasting set.

He peered out through the door. From where he sat he could see nothing of the gangsters. He could hear the buzz of their voices and an occasional clatter of a plate, but that was all.

Collins slumped forward. It was useless to try. He gave way to the pain which was shooting through his skull and the ugly ache which was creeping up his arms.

Something tugged at his nostrils. An odor he had not before noticed. Absently he catalogued it. Cigarette butts burning in an ashtray. Then he stiffened and glanced to the left.

Not two feet from his elbow stood a high ashtray. He suddenly recalled the burning match which Tascori had thrown into it. The pile of butts was smoldering red coals, showing through the gray ashes.

Hope leaped up in his breast. Cautiously, lest his chair scrape loudly on the floor, he hitched the chair toward the ashtray. Inch by inch he closed the gap. Finally, sweat standing out on his brow from the exertion, he managed to touch one of the strips to the smouldering heap.

A coal touched his wrist and he flinched. Then, gritting his teeth, he shoved the cloth back into the smoke. Gradually he could feel the cloth loosen. The burning fabric seared up his wrist, but he bit his lip and held it there.

The next instant his left hand was free! Feverishly, praying for time, he tore at the bonds of his right hand.

At any minute Tascori or one of his men might return to the room and discover him. The hand came free. He twisted his numb hands together for an instant and then snatched at his feet. The knots there were stubborn and held out for long, precious seconds against his onslaught. He gave one last jerk and his feet were free.

Unsteadily he jumped to his feet. Stinging pains shot up through his legs. He stepped gingerly forward. Then there came an overwhelming impulse to run and he gave way to it.

A door stood in back of the chair and he silently pulled it open, expecting to see another room or a hall. He darted into the dark doorway and then stopped. He had entered a closet.

Turning, he glanced wildly about the room. But the door which led to the gangsters was the only other entrance. And to cross the room to the stairs meant discovery.

Running a numb hand across his forehead impatiently, he turned back to the radios. Again he caught sight of the open switch, the unattached mike leads. On tiptoe he crossed the room, and drew the two microphones from his pocket and laid them on the table. He snatched up his coat and drew the coils of wire from it. His hands were stiff and clumsy, but they quickly wrapped the leads together.

He cursed his lack of pliers as he attempted to cut the excess wire which hung to the tiny microphone, but even though the wire was small, it hung stubbornly together.

Failing in this, he was forced to join the leads with the twenty-foot strips which composed the coils. He was about to throw the switch down when a sudden hunch took hold of him.

Taking the other small mike, he lashed it to the receiving set beside the broadcaster. It was the work of half a minute.

Then pulling out the long wires so that they would not short, he laid the two mikes side by side on the table top. Deftly he tuned the broadcasting set by its numbered dials. His hand swept out toward the switch. At that instant he heard a chair scrape in the outer room. His heart seemed to stop beating and his hand stopped in midair. With a sob he threw on the switch. He whirled to the receiver and clicked on its juice. A footstep rang against boards in the other room.

The footsteps were coming closer. Collins swept the two small mikes into his pocket, and darted back to his chair. With a jerk of his arm he threw all four wires back along the wall, almost out of sight.

Just as his hand came back alongside the chair, Tascori stepped through the open door. He noticed nothing unusual at first. In fact he hardly glanced at the radioman. He paused in the middle of the room to light a cigarette.

The slam of a door crashed through the house. Tascori started violently and he stared with his one eye fixed on the door he had just stepped through.

A heavy footfall followed the slamming of the door.

The sound came from the back of the house. Tascori spun about and whipped an automatic from his pocket. Holding it by the barrel, he darted to Collins. It was not until then that he noticed the absence of the bonds and the telltale cloth on the floor.

With an oath he brought the butt of the automatic against the radioman's head with a terrific smash. Collins tried to dodge, but too late, and he caught the full force of the blow over his ear. Darkness crashed down upon him.

Tascori grabbed at the radioman's shirtfront and half-dragged, half-pitched him through the open closet door. Collins sank down, to all appearances dead. A new trickle of blood was flowing onto the closet floor. Tascori closed the closet and thrust the gun back in his pocket. Quickly assuming a nonchalant air, he walked to the entrance of the room. A tall figure was approaching him.

Suddenly Tascori swore and his eye kindled. "What do you mean bursting in here like that! Get this, Giovanni, you'll walk softly while you're in my gang or you'll be taking a little ride!"

Giovanni stopped and looked down at the floor. "I'm sorry, Tascori. But I was in a hurry to tell you the news."

"All right," snapped Tascori. "What is it?"

Tony and the three other gangsters came up beside him.

"Listen!" said Giovanni. "It ain't healthy to stick around here no longer."

Tascori stepped forward. "What do you mean?"

"Just this," Giovanni replied, "I saw a squad car parked a block down the street and I don't like it!"

Tony's jaw dropped. "A squad car! Maybe they know where to look for us!" He was tense with fear.

"Two blocks from here, eh?" Tascori's face was a calm mask. "Maybe you're right, Giovanni." He walked to the chair which had held Collins and tapped his fingers on its back. "All right. We'll get our stuff together and leave. We can cruise down the back alley out of sight. We can't afford to fight any cops right now." He started toward the stairs.

The shortwave receiver crackled.

"Huh!" said Tony. "I must have left it on this afternoon."

He started toward the table, his hand outstretched to snap the button. His fingers touched the metal. At that instant, the receiver spoke.

"Calling Squad Car Sixty-five. Calling Squad Car Sixty-five. Calling Squad Car Sixty-five."

The voice was somewhat muffled but very crisp. It held a nasal twang.

"New announcer," stated Tascori as he paused at the foot of the stairs. "Let's see what he says. That's probably the one you saw outside, Giovanni."

Giovanni nodded his head in affirmation.

"Calling Squad Car Sixty-five," intoned the loudspeaker. "Proceed immediately to 622 South Hanover Street. Six, two, two, South Hanover Street. Proceed to six, two, two, South Hanover Street. Prowler reported nearby. Prowler reported nearby. Proceed immediately."

The radio fell silent and Tony was reaching for the button when it spoke again.

"Calling all squad cars in north of city. Calling all squad cars in north of city." The voice was monotonous. "Calling all squad cars in north of city. Proceed in general direction of northern city limits.

"Proceed immediately north to intercept Tascori mob. Attention all squad cars in north of city. 'One-Eye' Tascori has been sighted at Dickerson and Spring Streets proceeding in general direction of Butler Square."

The radio droned on, assigning streets to cars, laying down a perfect net to trap the reported gangster.

Tascori laughed shortly. “Dumb cops! I guess we’ll stay right here tonight. Safe enough with them chasing us all over the other side of town. Leave it on. I want another good laugh like that one!”

He tugged at the patch over his sightless eye and came back into the room. Picking up a paper, he once more read the story of Collins’ downfall. Then, lying back in an upholstered chair, he lit a cigarette and inhaled deeply.

For a good half hour he stared ahead of him, plans passing back and forth behind his narrowed eye. Suddenly he snapped out of his reverie.

The front door had slammed! Feet were heard running through the house! In the other room the gangsters threw back their chairs and jerked at their automatics. Tascori sprang up, balanced for an instant on the balls of his feet and then ran for the door.

But a drawling voice stopped him. He glanced about him and then stared at the receiving set.

“You’d better stay where you are, Tascori!” It was the voice of Collins! “Police are all around the house and in the surrounding rooms. You’re trapped! You and the rest of your mob better surrender quietly if you want to live a few weeks longer!”

Tony and Giovanni had run to the door at the sound of the voice. They stared for a moment at the receiving set. Their guns fell from nerveless fingers and clattered to the floor.

Tascori swayed slightly and then insanely he sent a bullet

crashing through the closed door of the closet. He remembered where he had left Collins.

A cold voice above him jerked him upright. A Thompson submachine gun was covering him. "Drop that gun, Tascori!" The light glinted from a metal badge.

With a hoarse scream, Tascori threw up his gun and fired wildly at the upper landing.

Flame spurted from the machine gun. The impact of bullets hurled the gangster's body to the floor. The crash of a pistol burst from the other room, and was followed by a fusillade.

The three remaining gangsters cowered against the walls, whipped.

The police chief walked down the stairs followed by two officers with the submachine gun. Four policemen stepped through the doorway and looked around. The chief glanced into the other room and then back at the stairs.

"Collins!" he called. "Where are you?"

The torn loudspeaker crackled for a moment and then was still. The chief stared at it, and then his keen eyes caught the almost invisible strands of wire which led from its back along the wall and under the closet door. He stepped to the place where they disappeared and threw back the door.

Motioning one of the officers to follow him, he entered and lifted Collins by the shoulders. The policemen picked up the limp legs and together they carried him to the upholstered chair.

As he sank back into the cushions, Collins opened his eyes.

Flame spurted from the machine gun. The impact of bullets hurled the gangster's body to the floor.

"I see you got my message." He smiled up at the gruff chief's face which was creased with wonder.

"Yes!" returned the chief. "You bet I did. How you got it to me I don't know, but I do know that you've done a wonderful night's work."

Collins opened his clutched hand. In it lay the two tiny microphones, and away from it ran the small strands of copper wire.

"It was just luck," he said weakly. "I finished these yesterday. Meant to have some fun with them at home by hooking them to our receiving set there. And when I came away from headquarters I took everything that belonged to me. Mainly these and some of this coil wire."

"Yes!" stammered the chief. "But how in the name of blazes did you get them hooked up?"

"Got loose while I was alone in the room, snapped them onto the sets. Meant to send the message right then, but I didn't have time. Why I attached this to the receiving set I don't know. Guess it was just because it was built for a receiving set.

"When I woke up in the closet I heard them talking and discovered these things in my pocket." He looked up at the chief, his drawn face was full of expectancy. "Listen. See that squad car map and that broadcasting set? There's your mystery of the unrecorded calls. They came from that set, and Tascori," he jerked his thumb at the prostrate body, "imitated my voice and gave out orders in the lull of headquarters' announcements. That's the answer. Listen, Chief, do I get my old job back?"

"Do you get your job back!" The chief started to slap Collins on the shoulder and then recalled that the man was injured. He changed the slap to a gentle pat.

"My boy, you can have the whole police force for this night's work! Come on, now we've got to get you to a doctor."

THE GREASE SPOT

THE GREASE SPOT

THE battered phonograph horn which served as a loudspeaker on the grimed wall rasped out the police message.

"Calling Car Seventy-five. Calling Car Seventy-five. Proceed to Tenth and Lynch Boulevard and investigate report of wreck."

Bill Milan uncoiled an incredible pair of long legs and stood up, reaching for his hat. His fat mechanic, Joe Pagett, scowled.

"You ain't going, are you, Bill?" growled Pagett.

"Sure I am. Don't think I'm scared, do you?"

"No. Sure you ain't scared, Bill. But just the same, when the bulls tell us that it means a year in the can, I'm thinkin' it ain't such a shiny idea to answer those wreck calls."

"Well, we've got to keep in business, haven't we?"

Joe Pagett nodded. "Yeah. We've got to keep in business, but just the same, I don't think the cops were fooling when they told us to lay off their private radio system. The chief sounded pretty sore."

Bill Milan slapped his hat on a head of tangled blond hair and grinned.

"It's worth the chance anyway, isn't it? If we don't pick up all the wreck business we can get, Bill Milan's Wrecker, Inc., is going to go all-fired broke. And if the cops are willing to shoot all the dope into the night air that way, what's the law against us going out after the business? Did you ever hear of any?"

Joe Pagett pursed his dubious lips and rubbed his palms against greasy coverall legs and sighed. "I know there ain't no laws about it, Bill, and I'm just the mechanic around here, but I'd hate like the very devil to see you cooling your heels in that bug-infested jail they've got in this town. Maybe it'd be different if they was a good calaboose here."

Bill Milan went to the door, paused, looking out into the rain which skittered across the black pavement. "Aw, those cops give me a pain. They're jealous, that's all."

"Okay, Bill," said Pagett. "It won't be me in the jail. But the least you can do is to drive slow and give those coppers a chance to get there first. And don't use that siren. They don't like that either."

Bill Milan shoved the garage door back and climbed into the ancient Fiat. The onetime limousine had been converted into a fast truck, and though its cab sat twice as high as any ordinary car, under Bill's competent hands the speed of the contrivance was astonishing.

He shot it out of the garage and skidded it to a stop in front of the door. The great cylinders scattered sparks down the exhaust stacks, but above their bellow, the loudspeaker, still bringing in the police broadcast, was easily heard.

"All cars. All cars," crackled the radio. "Drop search for

Carbonelli and companion. They have been reported crossing the state line fifteen minutes ago and are now outside our jurisdiction. This is radio station PXQ."

The Fiat's cylinders blasted out a throaty roar. Bill Milan stamped on the accelerator and rocketed out to the black, shining pavement. His windshield wiper was going across his line of vision, and through the clear arc, the street lights began to lope past. The tires sang over the wet asphalt. His fingers sought for and found the string which led to the siren under the cowl. The rising scream of the nickel barrel began to clear the traffic for a swaying, yowling truck. Bill Milan was headed for Tenth and Lynch Boulevard.

The deftness of Bill's saber-swift driving was not without its reason. Only two years before, Bill Milan had taken the Indianapolis track for a record. He had barreled and bent his streaking bus five hundred miles to a new low time. But now, Bill Milan's long right leg sometimes refused to move when he wanted it worst. That had come from a badly mended break. The track doctors had told Bill his racing career was done. That had been that. But there was still a thrill in lashing the lurching Fiat out across the streets of the city. Especially through the battering rain.

For a while after the finish of his high-speed career, Bill Milan's fast driving had been profitable. He had found that the police always broadcast wreck locations to their squad cars, and Bill had used that fact to the limit. The loudspeaker on his wall always told him where to go and when to go, and as a consequence, he had minted money. Always the first wrecker there, he got the business.

But the phenomenon of Bill's presence at the scene of every wreck had begun to cause not a little comment. It had gone too far to be accredited to mere luck. And the rival towing companies had ferreted out the secret. Even then, however, they stood little chance. The first man on the scene was the man hired. And Bill's racing tactics, even when applied to a rumbling, bellowing tow truck, were something to be reckoned with.

Up to that point, the police had not cared. But as Bill progressed, it seemed that he had acquired the habit of beating the squad cars to the scene. And that, because it directly reflected upon the ability and efficiency of the department, was bad. Bill had been summarily forbidden to utilize the radio to locate his wrecks upon the pain of a severe fine and even more severe sentence.

Tenth and Lynch Boulevard met at an angle near the city limits. Only street lights gleamed. The ghosts of darkened houses haunted the background of the highway. It was from one of those that the call had come, for certainly no one stood about the wrecked machine.

Bill skidded to a stop and looked down into the ditch. The car's nose was crumpled against the far bank. Segments of the white rail jutted out through the motor's base. The front wheels had torn loose from the inverted body and lay alone and smashed fifty feet away. The taillight shone like a wet ruby.

"They must be dead," murmured Bill and climbed down. Out of the odds and ends in the back of the truck he took a heavy-duty lamp, and with this swinging at his side, he stumbled down the slippery bank and peered through the gaping rear window.

But no bodies were in sight. Bill scratched his head and looked up at the highway. He grinned a little when he realized that he had beaten the squad car again. Perhaps he had better drive off and wait for them to come up. Otherwise he'd be arrested probably.

He knew better than to move the wrecked car. There was something mysterious about it. A man didn't leave so flashy a machine even though it was wrecked badly.

Bill started to turn back, but something stopped him. A round, hard something which bruised his lean ribs. A thin, bitter face hovered over his shoulder, the black eyes hard. The face seemed to be suspended in midair, completely without support. The man's black topcoat finished the illusion.

"Just stand there!" rattled the man. "Put your hands up a little." He ran his fingers over Bill's pockets, frisking him for a gun. The sensation was like that of a snake crawling.

Another face came up on Bill's left. "I got him covered, Carbonelli. Get the stuff out of the bus and let's go."

"What's this?" inquired Bill.

"We're playing tag," snarled Carbonelli. "You're it. You made good time getting here, and I'll see to it that you make better time getting away. Bumping one more guy won't make no difference to us."

The other's voice was like the bite of acid. "Yeah, he'll drive us all right. And I'm glad, for one."

Carbonelli bristled. "You didn't help matters any by grabbing the emergency, you dumbhead."

"Yeah, but you put us in the ditch, didn't you? And right before the bulls cracked wise that we'd left the state. We had a clean chance to hide out right here."

Bill Milan could hear the radio still going in the wrecked car. It was faint and sputtering, but the words were distinct. Something about a woman thinking she'd heard a burglar in the house and would the police come up and investigate. Bill wondered that the radio still worked.

The two men were scowling at each other through the rain, their faces lighted by the beam from the wrecker. Their nerves were raw and their working jaw muscles were tight.

"Okay, Krone," grated Carbonelli. "Okay. When we get out of this we'll split up, get me? I'm sick of your face and sick of your lip. You bumped those guys and you didn't need to!"

Krone leaned forward as though about to strike. His gun shifted away from Milan and covered Carbonelli. "I ain't in the bank business for my health, pally. Get that and get it right. We got the stuff, didn't we? And we got it because I bumped those guards. All right, shut up!"

Bill Milan, unobserved, swayed back a little. His hands came slowly down to shoulder height. His fists were hard knots. Standing as he was between the pair and the headlights of the wrecker, his movements passed unobserved. With the sudden intensity of lightning, he struck. Krone took it on the side of the jaw and went down, crying out.

Carbonelli brought up a glittering gun. Bill kicked it away and waded in. His fists sought Carbonelli's chest. They rocked the hard-faced bandit like a sledgehammer rocks a thin stake. Years of battling a fighting wheel had given Bill Milan such muscles.

Carbonelli backed up. His fists were futile, useless things. His eyes were no longer hard. They were lit with a fear of physical pain.

Milan followed him up. The bank was at Carbonelli's heels, muddy and slick. The rain battered their faces, blinded them. Milan tensed himself for one last haymaker.

With dismaying abruptness, his weak leg caved in. Bill tottered to one side, off his balance, fighting to hold himself erect. He swore through gritted teeth.

Carbonelli's eyes lighted with savage fire. He shot out his foot and smashed at Milan's shoulder. Bill slipped and thudded into the oozing mud. An instant later Carbonelli dropped on him. Krone rolled over and caught Bill's legs, holding them with both arms as a football player grabs a tackling dummy. Carbonelli's fists spattered against Milan's unprotected features.

"Okay," rattled Krone. "Okay. He'll drive now."

"You bet he'll drive," agreed Carbonelli. "And when we get to the end of the road we'll fix it so he'll never leave a clue as to what finished him." He smiled, a thin, evil twitch of his blackish lips. "If we put him out of the way so he can't be identified, we won't leave any trail and the first report will stand. Get me?"

"Yeah. But for God's sake, get going. The bulls'll be here in about two seconds."

Carbonelli kicked Bill Milan awake. He dragged him to the top of the bank and made Bill stand up. "You're going to drive us," stated Carbonelli, "and no more monkey business."

Bill's face tightened. His blue eyes were watchful. "Okay with me."

They climbed into the cab. Bill started the engine and shot the truck into gear. It rumbled forward, one wheel off the pavement. Its stiff springs let the body jolt. Bill threw out the clutch.

"I think I got a flat," he said.

Carbonelli growled, "Get out there and see, Krone."

"To hell with you!" snapped Krone. "I ain't going back into that rain again. Not for anything. Let him go. He ain't got the guts to try to take a powder on us."

Bill climbed down gingerly because of his leg. He knew that the truck ran that way naturally, but the two bandits didn't know it. They were used to easy passenger cars. He made his way around to the back, then limped up to the front. There he boosted himself up to the seat and slammed the door.

"I was wrong," he stated.

"Yeah, a stall, huh?" Carbonelli lifted his retrieved gun. "Get going and get going fast. I hear a squad car coming."

The Fiat rocketed away. The motor yammered and the tires howled over the wet asphalt. The last of the street lights disappeared with the white city limit sign.

Carbonelli kicked Bill Milan awake. He dragged him to the top of the bank and made Bill stand up. "You're going to drive us," stated Carbonelli, "and no more monkey business."

Bill's rugged face was etched by the slanted panel light. His hatless head was buffeted by the wind which blasted into his window. His strong hands handled the heavy wheel as though it were made of light paper. The speedometer went up to sixty and stopped. Beyond that it did not register.

"Want me to run without lights?" he asked.

"What you trying to do?" rasped Krone. "Get us picked up?"

"No—I was just trying to be helpful, that's all."

"I'll bet!" snapped Krone from the far side of the cab. "You're hoping some bicycle bull will spot us. If one does, and you don't act right, both you and him will be kissing angels."

A darkened farm slid by occasionally. The highway unwound like a black snake uncoiling. The rises were dark pits into which the headlights dipped. The white railings fluttered by, echoing the motor's roar through the cuts.

Above the windshield an old alarm clock swung uneasily by a string, ticking faintly. The hands pointed to midnight and then crept on around to two o'clock.

Krone was nervous. Holding a satchel on his knees, he stared back down the road, watching for possible pursuit. He gave Carbonelli's shoulder a convulsive grip.

"There's a cop!" he grated. And to Bill, "Step on it, you!"

"No!" rapped Carbonelli. "Slow down and let him come up. If we keep on running, he'll have us stopped in a town."

Bill Milan slowed down. The motorcycle's headlight lanced out in front of them, throwing their shadow. It swung close. Milan pulled over to the side and stopped. He could feel Carbonelli's leg muscles tighten. The bandit's gun was masked by his topcoat.

The officer stopped and threw his leg over the gas tank of his mount. With slow, deliberate movements, he leaned the motorcycle against the truck's running board. He drew off his gloves without looking into the cab. Then he extracted his book from a breast pocket and fluttered the pages. Rain dripped down his slicker, running from the peak of his rubber-covered hat.

"Driver's license, please," he said.

Bill handed it over.

The officer began to copy the name down on a ticket. When he had finished making it out, he handed the license back. Bill took the ticket and examined it.

The officer took the number from the front license plate and wrote it down. Then he asked for the ticket back and put another check on it.

"One headlamp is out," he announced. "And your taillight isn't burning. You wrecking guys may get away with speeding, but you got to have lights, understand? Get 'em fixed up at the next service station and after this watch 'em."

"Okay," said Bill. He wiped his palm on the side of his leg and somehow lost the ticket. It fluttered down to the floor. Bill reached for it, feeling around the base of the gearshift lever, using his left hand, which was awkward.

"Where you headed for?" demanded the state policeman.

"Guy stuck in the ditch about ten miles up the road," said Bill. "I'm on the . . . I'm . . ." He swallowed nervously. He put his left hand on the outside of the cab and lifted it in an expression of what's-the-use. "I mean I'm on my way to get him out, see?"

The officer nodded. "Remember to get those headlights fixed, understand?" He kicked his motorcycle into life and turned it around, heading back down the road through the rain.

Bill Milan sighed and started up again.

"You shoulda seen that when you got out to look at the tire," accused Krone. "I oughta bump you for that."

"The rain shorted it out," said Bill defensively.

Carbonelli snorted. "Well, you put on a pretty good act, anyway."

The Fiat lurched ahead. The clock above the windshield swung back and forth, jerkily. The odds and ends in the back rattled and clanked in tune with the dripping chain hoist. Bill Milan's hands were tense on the wheel. He eased off on the accelerator before they hit the curves, and then before their inertia could throw them off the poorly banked road, he shot the gas to the bellowing engine and blasted out into the straightaway. The wheels caressed the shoulders in repeated skids, but each time Bill brought the truck back with throttle and steering gear. He was driving as only a race driver is capable of driving.

Carbonelli's face was white in the light of the panel. Krone, though he continued to look back occasionally, watched the road ahead with a strained expression. Krone held both satchel and door side. Each time they roared around a curve, Krone's feet pressed hard against the floorboard as he put on the mental brakes.

"Hell!" cried Carbonelli. "I can't stand it anymore. I can't, I tell you! Stop this thing!"

Krone shook his head. "They'll catch up with us if we stop now."

"That's all right. We'll stop. There's an old house down in the woods on the next hill. We'll stop there. And don't try nothing, guy, when we do, see?" he snarled at Milan.

"I can't pull off into the mud!" said Bill. "We'll get stuck."

"Don't worry none about that," growled Krone. "Just pull off to the side of the road and park for a few minutes. That's all."

"And don't forget to fix them lights," warned Carbonelli, shifting his gun.

Bill slammed on the brakes. The heavy truck skidded to the right. He fed it the throttle and straightened it out. He slammed the brakes on again.

"What you trying to do?" screamed Carbonelli. "Kill us?"

For answer, Bill hit the muddy shoulder and clamped a hand around the emergency. The back of the truck slued around, making a long, wide gash in the muck. They stopped. Both Carbonelli and Krone sighed with relief.

"Don't forget them lights," again said Carbonelli.

Bill climbed down. "I'll have to hook this flashlamp to the rear for a red light," he said. "It's got a red bulb in it."

"Then snap into it," growled Krone. And when Bill disappeared around to the end of the truck, he muttered to Carbonelli, "This guy is a pipe. Dumb as they make 'em. We won't waste much time bumping him."

"Naw," said Carbonelli. "I got it all figured out."

When Bill Milan had fixed the connection on the front headlamp, the two climbed down into the slanting drizzle and ordered him to walk down the narrow path toward the woods. But before he went, Bill reached back into the cab under the panel.

"What you doing?" demanded Krone.

"Fixing the light connection," said Bill. "That's what shorted those two lights out."

"Okay. But snap it up." Krone fidgeted, still clinging to the satchel.

Carbonelli searched through the back of the truck and finally brought forth some lengths of wire.

Bill started down the path, walking easily. The two followed him, glancing back, as watchful as a pair of jungle cats. Bill stopped before a low stone house and started to enter.

With a swift movement, Carbonelli darted up behind him. The gun butt swooped down, glittering in the light of Krone's flash. Bill saw the shadow of the weapon. He dodged sideward. Carbonelli swore and struck again. Bill whirled on him and struck out. Krone swung the heavy satchel. It whistled down and caught Bill between the shoulder blades.

Bill's breath sighed out of him. His knees buckled. He crunched down on his lame leg. Carbonelli followed up the satchel blow with a strike to the head with the gun. Bill sprawled in the mud.

"The damned fool thought we was just going to lock him up," said Krone. "Didn't he get the surprise of his life."

Carbonelli knelt and went to work with the iron wire. He tied Bill's wrists and ankles and then fastened them together down the back. "There's a river over there about a hundred feet," he said. "If we can find a log along the bank, nobody'll be able to tell just where he was thrown in."

"That's smart stuff—that's smart." Krone eyed the road nervously. He could see the lights of the truck. "But let's make it snappy."

Carbonelli picked up Bill's shoulders and dragged him down the sloping bank. The water was muttering along the banks, whipped by the rain. The stream was not large, but it was uniformly deep, deeper than a man's head. It ran almost perpendicular to the road and south from it. A floating burden might not come to rest for some miles, possibly near an entirely different highway.

Krone found the log. It was high on the grass, its bark slimy with water. Krone threw his shoulders into it and rolled it down close to the water's edge. With Carbonelli's help he launched one end.

They tied Bill with his back against the log. Bill's head lolled to one side, the blond hair streaming damply into the black water. With a grunt, Krone thrust the log out into the stream. Almost immediately, it rolled over, placing Bill's face beneath the surface. The current caught at the wood and whirled it away beyond the range of Krone's flashlight.

They turned and plodded up the bank toward the car. The lamp that Bill had placed at the rear made the mud glow red.

Bill Milan came alive at the first touch of the water. Instinctively, he drew in a long breath before his head rolled under. But before he could collect himself enough to hold the air in his lungs, he expelled it in a gasp of dismay. He fought to free his wrists, but the wire buried itself in his flesh.

The log rolled, allowing him to get another breath of air. His face was shoved under once more. This time he held his breath, waiting for the log to roll. After seconds, each one an hour long, the tree trunk shifted unsteadily. Bill caught his third gulp of air. But he knew that this could not last. Sooner or later the log would roll the wrong way and he would be under long enough to lose consciousness. After that—well, there wasn't any use to worry about that.

Bill went to work on the wire. He wondered what kind it was. If it happened to be copper he stood but little chance of breaking it by bending. He made himself pull his wrists at different angles. The torture was unbearable, but he kept on. The log shifted, dragged back and forth by the stream, caught in eddies and released again. The rain ruffled the surface. The night was blacker than ink. Unseen, the bank went by slowly.

His wrists were bleeding, raw. His mind was whirling with the lack of oxygen. He gritted his teeth and tried to keep from getting panicky, working his wrists and trying to keep sane.

Abruptly his right hand came free. Immediately he stroked out and righted the tree trunk. After that he lay still, fanning the water to keep upright, thankful of the opportunity to breathe as much air as he wanted to breathe.

Bill Milan knew that he was not yet free. And besides that he had lost his only stock in trade, his wrecker. The last of the prize money he had won at Indianapolis had gone into his business and without the Fiat he was as good as ruined. But if he had figured right . . .

After a few minutes of rest, he was able to free his left hand. After that, he worked at his back until it too was unlashed. His ankles were easy. Silently, he slipped off the log and struck out for the shore he could not see.

With ground under his feet again, Bill put his hand in the water to determine the current and struck out upstream toward the stone house. The way was dark. He ran into trees, tripped through windfalls. He made as good time as possible, but even that time was slow. He had no idea how far he had gone in the river.

After a year of hours, he struck a trail and followed it. The going was better but he was continually losing the edge and finding it necessary to locate the path once more. The rain was giving way to a gray light in the east. Bill knew that it must be close to dawn. If he could make it before the sun came, he could . . .

The stone house sat in the middle of a small clearing. The first thing Bill saw was the outline of his truck. It had been clumsily hidden by chopped brush, but even in the darkness it was recognizable. The rain had almost ceased.

Bill stopped, crouching in the bushes, waiting for something to happen. And that something was not long in coming. Carbonelli came to the window and thrust his head out.

"I guess it's stopped raining," said the thug in a disgruntled voice.

"Sure," Krone's voice snapped from inside. "You said that an hour ago."

"Well, I can't help it, can I? We'll have to get that truck fixed as soon as it's dry enough to work on. Damn this rain! It must have shorted all the wires."

"That was a bright stunt of yours." Krone's voice growled nastily. "Some guy'll find that dumb driver and they'll trace back up this stream and nail us. I'm for clearing out of here on foot and trying to swipe a car in the next town."

"Why swipe one?" asked Carbonelli. "We can buy one or take a train. The cops ain't looking for us in this state now since they got a tip that we'd left here."

"All right, let's go."

Bill's heart was hammering. He had to keep these two here somehow. Under his hand lay a rock. He picked it up and heaved it at the window. The glass crashed out.

"What the hell?" shrieked Krone. "What was that?"

"A rock!" said Carbonelli in a high-pitched voice. "They've got us surrounded!"

Krone evidently regained some of his nerve. "Surrounded, my hat. They wouldn't have thrown that rock. They'd have shot you."

Neither of the two had quite the courage to go to the window again. Bill stood up and looked at the truck through the cold gray light. He gritted his teeth against the pain of his leg and raced across the clearing. He gained the cab before they heard him.

A bullet whined off a tree. The report was flat and dead.

Bill shot a hand under the panel and turned the petcock he had closed earlier in the evening. Then he jammed his foot down on the starter. The Fiat's engine roared away, plumes of blue smoke jumping from the exhaust stacks. Another bullet smashed through the side of the door, came all the way through.

Bill turned off the switch and turned it on again. The motor backfired. The sound was identical with that of exploding powder. He knew that the ruse would not last long. Soon they'd get over their first scare and they'd charge him.

Carbonelli threw open the door. His gun jumped. The windshield went out of the cab. Flying glass gashed Bill's cheek. He scuttled back and tried to open the other side of the cab. But a branch held it shut. Suddenly Bill knew that he was trapped. He could not get out and he had no way of protecting himself. They might not try to get in the doors for fear he had a gun, but one could keep him busy from the front while the other came through the back. He glanced out and saw the dangling chain hoist. A slug ripped through a wood beam and he ducked.

Krone approached warily from the front, crouching, ready to shoot. Carbonelli had disappeared. He would be coming around from the back.

Krone weaved from side to side. His gun flamed. His eyes were jets of black fire. Bill heard someone scrambling up the tailgate. That would be Carbonelli.

The idling motor sputtered and coughed. Bill stared at the panel on the level with his face, waiting. A lever came into his line of vision. The lever which operated the chain hoist.

Before he had time fully to think the plan out, Bill hauled back on the hand clutch.

The chain which hung over the back rattled. The winch screamed under the onslaught of the racing motor. A bellow of rage and dismay blasted through the dripping woods.

Carbonelli was caught. Caught like a fish on a hook. The hoist he had used to pull himself up had suddenly gone wild in his hands. The hook was through his coat collar. His feet danced on thin air.

Krone dodged. He started to charge and then stopped. A slow smile came over his twisted face. He lowered the gun and watched Carbonelli dance.

"Get me off of here!" shrieked Carbonelli. "He'll kill me! Get me off! I'm choking to death!"

Krone smiled again. He knew now that there was no danger from the front of the cab. He raised his gun slowly and sighted down the barrel. His intention was obvious. He was unwilling to share the contents of the satchel. Carbonelli was about to die.

But Krone had reckoned without the gun Carbonelli still clutched. Carbonelli's terror departed as swiftly as it had come. He saw the revolver coming up and he knew he was about to be killed. His own weapon jumped into a level position. His hand convulsed.

Krone's face was blank for an instant. He took a step forward, stumbling. Then a look of surprise swept over his features. He made one last movement and then, with the limpness of a falling sack, struck the ground.

Carbonelli's gun swung toward the cab. "All right, you!" he cried. "Let me down from here or I'll blast the back of the seat."

Bill slipped sideward and out the door. His intention was to make the road unseen. But the game leg was wobbly after the run and the ground was oozy with rain. He swerved out an inch too far.

Carbonelli saw him and shot him in the same instant.

The sun climbed higher and higher. No clouds were up there now. Only glazed blue sky. Bill struggled feebly from time to time, but he had just enough energy left to keep his hand clamped on the severed shoulder artery. He could see Carbonelli's dangling legs and he could hear Carbonelli's vituperation.

Bill waited for the help he knew would come.

It was nine o'clock before the state and city officers arrived. They came with sirens and whistles open wide. They swarmed down the wood road like an avalanche. A dozen guns covered the swearing Carbonelli. A dozen hard faces stared at the earthly remains of Krone, the coldblooded killer.

When the police first-aid kit had been ransacked for tourniquets and probes and Merthiolate, and when Bill sat propped up against a tree, the reporters and photographers were there, bubbling with eager questions. They fortified Bill Milan with a drink, a big drink, because they suddenly remembered that, two years before, Bill Milan had been the hottest man on any track in the country.

A hard-boiled reporter with a cigarette dangling from his lips said, "All right. We know the police facts about the bank robbery and all. We want your story straight through."

Bill smiled, took another drink and complied. "It was pretty simple. I knew they would try to get rid of me sooner or later and I had to use my head. So when we started out I said we had a flat and went around back and disconnected the rear light. I also turned out a headlight. I knew that their absence would pick up a cop because they've been pretty strict about it lately.

"Then, when the policeman turned up, I had to let him know I was in trouble. He was smart. He ought to get a promotion out of it. I wiped off my hand and reached down to the bottom of the gearshift. By rubbing my palm there, I made a perfect black circle. I said I was on the—and then didn't finish it with words. I waved my hand and he caught on. That circle made a white spot on my hand. He got it. I was on—the spot, see? I knew then that the police would start to look for my truck.

"When they made me stop up there on the highway, I slued my wheels so they'd leave a big track, very noticeable in the mud. Then I turned off the gasoline so they could just start the truck and that was all. I knew then that they'd have to stay here. They didn't like the rain and I was pretty sure they wouldn't walk in it. Then I had to fix up the rear light according to their orders. So I took the heavy-duty lantern which had three bulbs—red, white and blue—and turned on the red bulb. I set the lantern on the ground, but they thought it was attached to the car. Then I wrote that message in the mud in front of the lantern for you fellows to find. You found it and that's all there is to it."

"Not all," said a captain of the city police, smiling. "We've reconsidered your feat of beating squad cars to the scene. If you want, you can do it anytime. And with the reward money the bank's offering, you will have enough to buy a fleet of cars. We'll give you exclusive rights to that. A sort of franchise."

"Thanks," said Bill through colorless lips. "That's mighty swell of you, Captain, but I want another favor."

"Sure, what?"

"Fix up those squad cars, will you, so they'll go faster? And have the police broadcast announce it when the squad car is almost on the scene. I tell you, Captain, I'm through with beating your boys to it. I'm in the wrecking business all right, but I'm damned if that means that I'm out to wreck myself!"

STORY PREVIEW

NOW that you've just ventured through some of the captivating tales in the Stories from the Golden Age collection by L. Ron Hubbard, turn the page and enjoy a preview of *Killer's Law.* Join Sheriff Kyle of Deadeye, Nevada, a straight shooter who finds treachery in the heart of Washington, DC when a senator is killed and he's accused of the murder.

KILLER'S LAW

WHEN Kyle stepped off the Capitol Limited and into the confused fury of Washington, a headline caught his glance:

SENATOR MORRAN BEGINS
COPPER QUIZ

A few hours from now, his own name would be blazing there, black as the ink in which it would be printed. Kyle knew nothing of prophecy; his interest was in getting through this stampede of people and completing his mission. Already he was creating a mild sensation. Palo Alto hat, silver thong, scarlet kerchief, high-heeled boots and his six feet three of gawky, bony height commanded attention.

He stood for a moment in the crowded, clanging dusk, looking toward the lighted dome of the Capitol, trying without much success to savor the scene and feel patriotic. A redcap, eyeing his huge bag now that Kyle had dragged it all the way through the station from the train, swooped down with confidence born of the stranger's obvious confusion. The action met abruptly explosive resistance.

Kyle said, "Hands off."

The redcap retained his hold as a legal right to a tip. Kyle gave the handle a twist which sent him reeling. A few people paused to watch.

A cop said, "What's the matter here? Keep moving, you."

Kyle said testily, "Move along, hell. I'm Sheriff Kyle of Deadeye, Nevada, and I got an appointment to meet Senator Morran—"

"Yeah?" the cop said.

"Could I be of assistance?" said a smooth-faced gentleman. "Your name, I think, is Kyle. Senator Morran sent me down to meet you." He laughed good-naturedly and nodded to the cop. "That's all right, Officer."

The cop was satisfied. The redcap departed without tip.

"My name is Johnson, Sheriff," the smooth-faced man said. "John Johnson. Just call me Johnny." He laughed. "And now we'll see about getting you to the senator."

"Hold it," Kyle said. "How do I know who you are?" He had to bend over to look at Johnson. He did so and said, "Why don't you just run along and tell the senator I'll be with him soon. I'm taking a cab."

"Well—" Johnson turned toward a waiting limousine and Kyle's glance collided with the chauffeur's. He moved away while Johnson still hesitated, and hailed a cab.

"Soreham Hotel," he told the driver.

The Soreham Hotel was lighted in every window, its walks aglitter with dinner gowns, its lobby thick with political cigar smoke and the aura of martinis. Kyle asked the desk clerk for the senator's room number and a house phone.

The phone didn't answer. He went up.

Senator Morran's room was 310. Its door, open to darkness, surprised Kyle. The faint hall light reached poorly into the room, but showed a dark, irregular streak, running jaggedly along the floor.

Kyle was in the act of stepping backward when the room exploded into Roman candle brilliance. The pain came fractionally later, just as the lights careened out again. His last conscious impression was of himself, trying to push the floor away with his hands.

GLOSSARY

GLOSSARY

STORIES FROM THE GOLDEN AGE *reflect the words and expressions used in the 1930s and 1940s, adding unique flavor and authenticity to the tales. While a character's speech may often reflect regional origins, it also can convey attitudes common in the day. So that readers can better grasp such cultural and historical terms, uncommon words or expressions of the era, the following glossary has been provided.*

---

apache: a gangster or thug. The term was first used in 1902 by a French journalist to describe a member of a gang of criminals in Paris noted for their crimes of violence. Their savagery was compared with the reputation the Europeans attributed to the Native American tribes of Apache Indians.

banshee: (Irish legend) a female spirit whose wailing warns of a death in a house.

be hanged: used to express exasperation or disgust.

blackjack: a short, leather-covered club, consisting of a heavy head on a flexible handle, used as a weapon.

bluecoats: policemen.

bo: pal; buster; fellow.

bullpen: a holding cell where prisoners are confined together temporarily; in the 1800s, jails and holding cells were nicknamed bullpens, in reference to many police officers' bullish features—strength and short temper.

bulls: cops; police officers.

bump: to kill.

calaboose: a jail.

cowl: the top portion of the front part of an automobile body, supporting the windshield and dashboard.

cretonne: a heavy cotton material in colorfully printed designs, used especially for drapery or slipcovers.

degree rooms: third-degree rooms; interrogation rooms; rooms of mental or physical torture used to obtain information or a confession from a prisoner.

dope: information, data or news.

drill: shoot.

excelsior: packing material made from wood shavings.

fire-eaters: firemen; firefighters.

flatfoot: a police officer; cop.

gat: a gun.

giddap: get up or go ahead.

gilt-frogged: garment with gold-colored ornamental fasteners consisting of a loop of braid and button or knot that fits into the loop.

G-men: government men; agents of the Federal Bureau of Investigation.

gone: provided (bail) for an arrested person.

hard-boiled: tough; unsentimental.

haymaker: a powerful blow with the fist.

jack: money.

jig's up, the: it's all over; usually referring to a scam, trick or plot that has been found out and foiled before it could come to fruition.

kerchief: handkerchief.

Merthiolate: a trademark name for thimerosal, a cream-colored crystalline powder used as a local antiseptic for abrasions and minor cuts.

mitts: hands.

mouthpiece: a lawyer, especially a criminal lawyer.

mugs: hoodlums; thugs; criminals.

nickel barrel: siren, from the outside cylindrical part or casing of a siren that is nickel plated or colored.

Palo Alto hat: a wide-brimmed slouch hat with a chinstrap most commonly worn as part of a military uniform, resembling the original Stetson that was called "Boss of the Plains."

petcock: a small valve used to control the flow of gas.

pile out: to move out.

pipe: cinch; someone or something that is easy and presents no problems.

pipe the dick: to look at or notice the detective.

powder, take a: to make a speedy departure; run away.

put ya wise: tell you; give you the information.

queered: spoiled; ruined; put wrong.

ride, take for a: to take out in a car intending to murder.

right guy: good guy.

roadster: another name for a police car.

Roman candle: a type of fireworks giving off flaming colored balls and sparks.

rubber hose: a piece of hose made of rubber, used to beat people as a form of torture or in order to obtain a full or partial confession and to elicit information. A rubber hose was used because its blows, while painful, leave only slight marks on the body of the person beaten.

sand blotting box: a box with a perforated top containing fine sand for sprinkling on wet ink. After absorbing and drying the ink, the sand was poured back into the blotting box to be used again.

sap: blackjack; a short, leather-covered club, consisting of a heavy head on a flexible handle, used as a weapon.

sapped: knocked out with a blackjack.

Scheherazade: the female narrator of *The Arabian Nights,* who during one thousand and one adventurous nights saved her life by entertaining her husband, the king, with stories.

slug: a bullet.

smoke-eaters: firemen.

speakeasy: a bar for the illegal sale and consumption of alcoholic drinks.

spokes: the rods that join the edge of the steering wheel to its center.

Stetson: as the most popular broad-brimmed hat in the West, it became the generic name for *hat.* John B. Stetson was a master hatmaker and founder of the company that has been making Stetsons since 1865.

Thompson submachine gun: a type of machine gun that fires short pistol rounds; named after its creator, John Taliaferro Thompson, who produced the first model in 1919.

uncle: surrender; indicate a willingness to give up a fight.

L. Ron Hubbard in the Golden Age of Pulp Fiction

In writing an adventure story
a writer has to know that he is adventuring
for a lot of people who cannot.
The writer has to take them here and there
about the globe and show them
excitement and love and realism.
As long as that writer is living the part of an
adventurer when he is hammering
the keys, he is succeeding with his story.

Adventuring is a state of mind.
If you adventure through life, you have a
good chance to be a success on paper.

Adventure doesn't mean globe-trotting,
exactly, and it doesn't mean great deeds.
Adventuring is like art.
You have to live it to make it real.

—L. RON HUBBARD

L. Ron Hubbard and American Pulp Fiction

BORN March 13, 1911, L. Ron Hubbard lived a life at least as expansive as the stories with which he enthralled a hundred million readers through a fifty-year career.

Originally hailing from Tilden, Nebraska, he spent his formative years in a classically rugged Montana, replete with the cowpunchers, lawmen and desperadoes who would later people his Wild West adventures. And lest anyone imagine those adventures were drawn from vicarious experience, he was not only breaking broncs at a tender age, he was also among the few whites ever admitted into Blackfoot society as a bona fide blood brother. While if only to round out an otherwise rough and tumble youth, his mother was that rarity of her time—a thoroughly educated woman—who introduced her son to the classics of Occidental literature even before his seventh birthday.

But as any dedicated L. Ron Hubbard reader will attest, his world extended far beyond Montana. In point of fact, and as the son of a United States naval officer, by the age of eighteen he had traveled over a quarter of a million miles. Included therein were three Pacific crossings to a then still mysterious Asia, where he ran with the likes of Her British Majesty's agent-in-place

L. Ron Hubbard, left, at Congressional Airport, Washington, DC, 1931, with members of George Washington University flying club.

for North China, and the last in the line of Royal Magicians from the court of Kublai Khan. For the record, L. Ron Hubbard was also among the first Westerners to gain admittance to forbidden Tibetan monasteries below Manchuria, and his photographs of China's Great Wall long graced American geography texts.

Upon his return to the United States and a hasty completion of his interrupted high school education, the young Ron Hubbard entered George Washington University. There, as fans of his aerial adventures may have heard, he earned his wings as a pioneering barnstormer at the dawn of American aviation. He also earned a place in free-flight record books for the longest sustained flight above Chicago. Moreover, as a roving reporter for *Sportsman Pilot* (featuring his first professionally penned articles), he further helped inspire a generation of pilots who would take America to world airpower.

Immediately beyond his sophomore year, Ron embarked on the first of his famed ethnological expeditions, initially to then untrammeled Caribbean shores (descriptions of which would later fill a whole series of West Indies mystery-thrillers). That the Puerto Rican interior would also figure into the future of Ron Hubbard stories was likewise no accident. For in addition to cultural studies of the island, a 1932–33

LRH expedition is rightly remembered as conducting the first complete mineralogical survey of a Puerto Rico under United States jurisdiction.

There was many another adventure along this vein: As a lifetime member of the famed Explorers Club, L. Ron Hubbard charted North Pacific waters with the first shipboard radio direction finder, and so pioneered a long-range navigation system universally employed until the late twentieth century. While not to put too fine an edge on it, he also held a rare Master Mariner's license to pilot any vessel, of any tonnage in any ocean.

Capt. L. Ron Hubbard in Ketchikan, Alaska, 1940, on his Alaskan Radio Experimental Expedition, the first of three voyages conducted under the Explorers Club flag.

Yet lest we stray too far afield, there is an LRH note at this juncture in his saga, and it reads in part:

"I started out writing for the pulps, writing the best I knew, writing for every mag on the stands, slanting as well as I could."

To which one might add: His earliest submissions date from the summer of 1934, and included tales drawn from true-to-life Asian adventures, with characters roughly modeled on British/American intelligence operatives he had known in Shanghai. His early Westerns were similarly peppered with details drawn from personal experience. Although therein lay a first hard lesson from the often cruel world of the pulps. His first Westerns were soundly rejected as lacking the authenticity of a Max Brand yarn (a particularly frustrating comment given L. Ron Hubbard's Westerns came straight from his Montana homeland, while Max Brand was a mediocre New York poet named Frederick Schiller Faust, who turned out implausible six-shooter tales from the terrace of an Italian villa).

Nevertheless, and needless to say, L. Ron Hubbard persevered and soon earned a reputation as among the most publishable names in pulp fiction, with a ninety percent placement rate of first-draft manuscripts. He was also among the most prolific, averaging between seventy and a hundred thousand words a month. Hence the rumors that L. Ron Hubbard had redesigned a typewriter for faster keyboard action and pounded out manuscripts on a continuous roll of butcher paper to save the precious seconds it took to insert a single sheet of paper into manual typewriters of the day.

That all L. Ron Hubbard stories did not run beneath said byline is yet another aspect of pulp fiction lore. That is, as publishers periodically rejected manuscripts from top-drawer authors if only to avoid paying top dollar, L. Ron Hubbard and company just as frequently replied with submissions under various pseudonyms. In Ron's case, the

A Man of Many Names

Between 1934 and 1950, L. Ron Hubbard authored more than fifteen million words of fiction in more than two hundred classic publications. To supply his fans and editors with stories across an array of genres and pulp titles, he adopted fifteen pseudonyms in addition to his already renowned L. Ron Hubbard byline.

Winchester Remington Colt
Lt. Jonathan Daly
Capt. Charles Gordon
Capt. L. Ron Hubbard
Bernard Hubbel
Michael Keith
Rene Lafayette
Legionnaire 148
Legionnaire 14830
Ken Martin
Scott Morgan
Lt. Scott Morgan
Kurt von Rachen
Barry Randolph
Capt. Humbert Reynolds

list included: Rene Lafayette, Captain Charles Gordon, Lt. Scott Morgan and the notorious Kurt von Rachen—supposedly on the lam for a murder rap, while hammering out two-fisted prose in Argentina. The point: While L. Ron Hubbard as Ken Martin spun stories of Southeast Asian intrigue, LRH as Barry Randolph authored tales of romance on the Western range—which, stretching between a dozen genres is how he came to stand among the two hundred elite authors providing close to a million tales through the glory days of American Pulp Fiction.

L. Ron Hubbard, circa 1930, at the outset of a literary career that would finally span half a century.

In evidence of exactly that, by 1936 L. Ron Hubbard was literally leading pulp fiction's elite as president of New York's American Fiction Guild. Members included a veritable pulp hall of fame: Lester "Doc Savage" Dent, Walter "The Shadow" Gibson, and the legendary Dashiell Hammett—to cite but a few.

Also in evidence of just where L. Ron Hubbard stood within his first two years on the American pulp circuit: By the spring of 1937, he was ensconced in Hollywood, adopting a Caribbean thriller for Columbia Pictures, remembered today as *The Secret of Treasure Island.* Comprising fifteen thirty-minute episodes, the L. Ron Hubbard screenplay led to the most profitable matinée serial in Hollywood history. In accord with Hollywood culture, he was thereafter continually called upon

The 1937 Secret of Treasure Island, *a fifteen-episode serial adapted for the screen by L. Ron Hubbard from his novel,* Murder at Pirate Castle.

to rewrite/doctor scripts—most famously for long-time friend and fellow adventurer Clark Gable.

In the interim—and herein lies another distinctive chapter of the L. Ron Hubbard story—he continually worked to open Pulp Kingdom gates to up-and-coming authors. Or, for that matter, anyone who wished to write. It was a fairly unconventional stance, as markets were already thin and competition razor sharp. But the fact remains, it was an L. Ron Hubbard hallmark that he vehemently lobbied on behalf of young authors—regularly supplying instructional articles to trade journals, guest-lecturing to short story classes at George Washington University and Harvard, and even founding his own creative writing competition. It was established in 1940, dubbed the Golden Pen, and guaranteed winners both New York representation and publication in *Argosy.*

But it was John W. Campbell Jr.'s *Astounding Science Fiction* that finally proved the most memorable LRH vehicle. While every fan of L. Ron Hubbard's galactic epics undoubtedly knows the story, it nonetheless bears repeating: By late 1938, the pulp publishing magnate of Street & Smith was determined to revamp *Astounding Science Fiction* for broader readership. In particular, senior editorial director F. Orlin Tremaine called for stories with a stronger *human element.* When acting editor John W. Campbell balked, preferring his spaceship-driven tales, Tremaine enlisted Hubbard. Hubbard, in turn, replied with the genre's first truly *character-driven* works, wherein heroes are pitted not against bug-eyed monsters but the mystery and majesty of deep space itself—and thus was launched the Golden Age of Science Fiction.

The names alone are enough to quicken the pulse of any science fiction aficionado, including LRH friend and protégé, Robert Heinlein, Isaac Asimov, A. E. van Vogt and Ray Bradbury. Moreover, when coupled with LRH stories of fantasy, we further come to what's rightly been described as the foundation of every modern tale of horror: L. Ron Hubbard's immortal *Fear.* It was rightly proclaimed by Stephen King as one of the very few works to genuinely warrant that overworked term "classic"—as in: *"This is a classic tale of creeping, surreal menace and horror. . . . This is one of the really, really good ones."*

L. Ron Hubbard, 1948, among fellow science fiction luminaries at the World Science Fiction Convention in Toronto.

To accommodate the greater body of L. Ron Hubbard fantasies, Street & Smith inaugurated *Unknown*—a classic pulp if there ever was one, and wherein readers were soon thrilling to the likes of *Typewriter in the Sky* and *Slaves of Sleep* of which Frederik Pohl would declare: *"There are bits and pieces from Ron's work that became part of the language in ways that very few other writers managed."*

And, indeed, at J. W. Campbell Jr.'s insistence, Ron was regularly drawing on themes from the Arabian Nights and so introducing readers to a world of genies, jinn, Aladdin and Sinbad—all of which, of course, continue to float through cultural mythology to this day.

At least as influential in terms of post-apocalypse stories was L. Ron Hubbard's 1940 *Final Blackout.* Generally acclaimed as the finest anti-war novel of the decade and among the ten best works of the genre ever authored—here, too, was a tale that would live on in ways few other writers imagined. Hence, the later Robert Heinlein verdict: "Final Blackout *is as perfect a piece of science fiction as has ever been written.*"

Portland, Oregon, 1943; L. Ron Hubbard, captain of the US Navy subchaser PC 815.

Like many another who both lived and wrote American pulp adventure, the war proved a tragic end to Ron's sojourn in the pulps. He served with distinction in four theaters and was highly decorated for commanding corvettes in the North Pacific. He was also grievously wounded in combat, lost many a close friend and colleague and thus resolved to say farewell to pulp fiction and devote himself to what it had supported these many years—namely, his serious research.

But in no way was the LRH literary saga at an end, for as he wrote some thirty years later, in 1980:

"Recently there came a period when I had little to do. This was novel in a life so crammed with busy years, and I decided to amuse myself by writing a novel that was pure *science fiction."*

That work was *Battlefield Earth: A Saga of the Year 3000.* It was an immediate *New York Times* bestseller and, in fact, the first international science fiction blockbuster in decades. It was not, however, L. Ron Hubbard's magnum opus, as that distinction is generally reserved for his next and final work: The 1.2 million word *Mission Earth.*

Final Blackout *is as perfect a piece of science fiction as has ever been written.*

—Robert Heinlein

How he managed those 1.2 million words in just over twelve months is yet another piece of the L. Ron Hubbard legend. But the fact remains, he did indeed author a ten-volume *dekalogy* that lives in publishing history for the fact that each and every volume of the series was also a *New York Times* bestseller.

Moreover, as subsequent generations discovered L. Ron Hubbard through republished works and novelizations of his screenplays, the mere fact of his name on a cover signaled an international bestseller. . . . Until, to date, sales of his works exceed hundreds of millions, and he otherwise remains among the most enduring and widely read authors in literary history. Although as a final word on the tales of L. Ron Hubbard, perhaps it's enough to simply reiterate what editors told readers in the glory days of American Pulp Fiction:

He writes the way he does, brothers, because he's been there, seen it and done it!

THE STORIES FROM THE GOLDEN AGE

Your ticket to adventure starts here with the Stories from the Golden Age collection by master storyteller L. Ron Hubbard. These gripping tales are set in a kaleidoscope of exotic locales and brim with fascinating characters, including some of the most vile villains, dangerous dames and brazen heroes you'll ever get to meet.

The entire collection of over one hundred and fifty stories is being released in a series of eighty books and audiobooks. For an up-to-date listing of available titles, go to www.goldenagestories.com.

AIR ADVENTURE

Arctic Wings
The Battling Pilot
Boomerang Bomber
The Crate Killer
The Dive Bomber
Forbidden Gold
Hurtling Wings
The Lieutenant Takes the Sky
Man-Killers of the Air
On Blazing Wings
Red Death Over China
Sabotage in the Sky
Sky Birds Dare!
The Sky-Crasher
Trouble on His Wings
Wings Over Ethiopia

FAR-FLUNG ADVENTURE

The Adventure of "X"
All Frontiers Are Jealous
The Barbarians
The Black Sultan
Black Towers to Danger
The Bold Dare All
Buckley Plays a Hunch
The Cossack
Destiny's Drum
Escape for Three
Fifty-Fifty O'Brien
The Headhunters
Hell's Legionnaire
He Walked to War
Hostage to Death
Hurricane
The Iron Duke
Machine Gun 21,000
Medals for Mahoney
Price of a Hat
Red Sand
The Sky Devil
The Small Boss of Nunaloha
The Squad That Never Came Back
Starch and Stripes
Tomb of the Ten Thousand Dead
Trick Soldier
While Bugles Blow!
Yukon Madness

SEA ADVENTURE

Cargo of Coffins
The Drowned City
False Cargo
Grounded
Loot of the Shanung
Mister Tidwell, Gunner
The Phantom Patrol
Sea Fangs
Submarine
Twenty Fathoms Down
Under the Black Ensign

TALES FROM THE ORIENT

The Devil—With Wings
The Falcon Killer
Five Mex for a Million
Golden Hell
The Green God
Hurricane's Roar
Inky Odds
Orders Is Orders
Pearl Pirate
The Red Dragon
Spy Killer
Tah
The Trail of the Red Diamonds
Wind-Gone-Mad
Yellow Loot

MYSTERY

The Blow Torch Murder
Brass Keys to Murder
Calling Squad Cars!
The Carnival of Death
The Chee-Chalker
Dead Men Kill
The Death Flyer
Flame City
The Grease Spot
Killer Ape
Killer's Law
The Mad Dog Murder
Mouthpiece
Murder Afloat
The Slickers
They Killed Him Dead

FANTASY

Borrowed Glory
The Crossroads
Danger in the Dark
The Devil's Rescue
He Didn't Like Cats
If I Were You
The Last Drop
The Room
The Tramp

SCIENCE FICTION

The Automagic Horse
Battle of Wizards
Battling Bolto
The Beast
Beyond All Weapons
A Can of Vacuum
The Conroy Diary
The Dangerous Dimension
Final Enemy
The Great Secret
Greed
The Invaders
A Matter of Matter
The Obsolete Weapon
One Was Stubborn
The Planet Makers
The Professor Was a Thief
The Slaver
Space Can
Strain
Tough Old Man
240,000 Miles Straight Up
When Shadows Fall

WESTERN

The Baron of Coyote River
Blood on His Spurs
Boss of the Lazy B
Branded Outlaw
Cattle King for a Day
Come and Get It
Death Waits at Sundown
Devil's Manhunt
The Ghost Town Gun-Ghost
Gun Boss of Tumbleweed
Gunman!
Gunman's Tally
The Gunner from Gehenna
Hoss Tamer
Johnny, the Town Tamer
King of the Gunmen
The Magic Quirt
Man for Breakfast
The No-Gun Gunhawk
The No-Gun Man
The Ranch That No One Would Buy
Reign of the Gila Monster
Ride 'Em, Cowboy
Ruin at Rio Piedras
Shadows from Boot Hill
Silent Pards
Six-Gun Caballero
Stacked Bullets
Stranger in Town
Tinhorn's Daughter
The Toughest Ranger
Under the Diehard Brand
Vengeance Is Mine!
When Gilhooly Was in Flower

In the Capital, All Trails Lead to Murder!

Sheriff Kyle of Deadeye, Nevada has traveled to the nation's capital to personally bring evidence against one of the state's wealthiest copper kings. But instead of giving his findings to the senator he's supposed to meet, Kyle discovers a trail of blood moments before he's knocked unconscious.

Kyle awakens to the flashing bulbs of reporters and harsh voices of police demanding to know why he's killed the popular politician. Things look particularly bleak—he's got no alibi, no memory of who knocked him out, and his five-inch knife is sticking out of the corpse—casting all suspicions his way.

Get

Killer's Law

Paperback or Audiobook: $9.95 each

Free Shipping & Handling for Book Club Members

Call toll-free: 1-877-8GALAXY (1-877-842-5299)

or go online to **www.goldenagestories.com**

Galaxy Press, 7051 Hollywood Blvd., Suite 200, Hollywood, CA 90028

JOIN THE PULP REVIVAL

America in the 1930s and 40s

Pulp fiction was in its heyday and 30 million readers were regularly riveted by the larger-than-life tales of master storyteller L. Ron Hubbard. For this was pulp fiction's golden age, when the writing was raw and every page packed a walloping punch.

That magic can now be yours. An evocative world of nefarious villains, exotic intrigues, courageous heroes and heroines—a world that today's cinema has barely tapped for tales of adventure and swashbucklers.

Enroll today in the Stories from the Golden Age Club and begin receiving your monthly feature edition selected from more than 150 stories in the collection.

You may choose to enjoy them as either a paperback or audiobook for the special membership price of $9.95 each month along with FREE shipping and handling.

CALL TOLL-FREE: **1-877-8GALAXY**
(1-877-842-5299) OR GO ONLINE TO
www.goldenagestories.com
AND BECOME PART OF THE PULP REVIVAL!

Prices are set in US dollars only. For non-US residents, please call 1-323-466-7815 for pricing information. Free shipping available for US residents only.

Galaxy Press, 7051 Hollywood Blvd., Suite 200, Hollywood, CA 90028